I0678760

KAMRAN SALAYEV

Elish and the Wicker Tales

London 2018

HERTFORDSHIRE PRESS

Published in United Kingdom
Hertfordshire Press Ltd © 2018
e-mail: publisher@hertfordshirepress.com
www.hertfordshirepress.com

ELISH AND THE WICKER TALES

original story by Kamran Salayev©

English

Translated & Illustrated by Timur Akhmedjanov
Edited by Gareth Stamp
Design by Aleksandra Vlasova

---

*All rights reserved. No part of this book may be reprinted or reproduced
or utilised in any form or by any electronic, mechanical, or other means,
now known or hereafter invented, including photocopying and recording,
or in any information storage or retrieval system, without permission in
writing from the publishers.*

*British Library Catalogue in Publication Data
A catalogue record for this book is available from the British Library
Library of Congress in Publication Data
A catalogue record for this book has been requested*

ISBN 978-1-910886-88-5
PAPREBACK RRP: £ 12.50

BRIDLE

PART ONE

In which our hero meets the Rider

I Want To Stay At Home

In the little village of Gyrusly there was only one street. However not a single villager would ever give it a name. Just a narrow strip of dirt, where no two waggons moving face to face could easily pass. The Street, for it is clear it has no actual name at all, began at the water spring and climbed up the hill to the other side of the village.

One day two young boys walked down to the water spring. They had arrived to a little house belonging to a boy simply known as Elish. The boys stopped at the step of the door. The older of the two went into the yard and, putting his fingers in his mouth, whistled loudly.

"Well?" Asked the the other one.

"I can't see him." replied the older boy.

"Hey, you can look in the barn, that's probably where he is!" Insisted the other boy.

"Elish!" Yelled the older boy. "Stop messing around with the twigs and strings and come with us to the upper meadow! They're going to play Chovgan there today!"

Inside the barn, stepping from the darkness, Elish cautiously approached the door leading to the world outside, however he did not open it, not even touch it. After all he felt more confident in the inviting darkness of the barn.

He gathered up the courage and peered suspiciously at the uninvited guests through the gap of the slightly open door.

"I'll probably stay home. I have to tie around twenty-four spider-hitch fishing knots and twine two braids until the day's finished." All those noisy people and buzzing crowds that will come to the game is something that did not appeal to him very much.

"Listen, Elish," the older one said trying to convince the stubborn boy. "Come with us today, and you can finish weaving your knots and braids tomorrow."

"I have other plans for tomorrow. I'll be trying to weave an asterisk pattern into the body of a fishtail-braid. If only you knew how difficult it really is!" Elish objected, hoping they would not understand him.

The boys looked at one another and shrugged their shoulders. Leaving, they whispered and giggled. Elish thought that they were chuckling at him as they left his yard. He turned around and stormed off quietly back inside, where a whole bunch of twigs and string were waiting, piled up on the cold ground of the lonely barn.

Anxiety

Elish took a willow twig from a bucket of water, inspected it, and twisting it into a ring, tested its strength. But as he was getting ready to weave the twig into a complex cross-shaped knot, his younger brother and sister rushed into the barn.

"Father is taking us on a fishing trip! Get ready! Hurry!" They cried with joy.

The small children grabbed him by the shoulders and begged him to go fishing with them. And from there it became quite clear for Elish that today was not the day he will finish the ambitious plans he had started.

"Perhaps you'll go without me?" He made his last attempt to stay in the barn but the younger brother and sister were inescapable.

"You what!" Sister shouted. "If you stay at home, father will not take us with him! Well, get a move on already!"

Elish laid the willow branch on the ground, sighed and silently followed them, pondering on how to connect a cross-shaped knot with a fishtail-braid. As the two siblings ran through the yard they stumbled upon their father.

"I'm glad you're coming with us Elish!" His father smiled as he noticed him tagging along behind his siblings. "I have a surprise for you all." The father pulled his hands from behind his back and there three fishing rods appeared before them.

"One fishing rod for each one of you." His father's eyebrows tightened as his gazed slightly hardened, as in trying to show that there will be no messing around on his watch.

However, his warning was not intended for Elish, but for the two shameless younglings who often robbed their elder brother of his things..

Fishing

Atop the riverbed of the Velvele river, which started its way high in the mountains, surrounded by the parting flow of the river, there laid a gigantic boulder in grandeur of all who stood before it. People believed that many centuries ago the terrible monster by the name of Ezhdah threw the boulder at the courageous hero, Demir the Fearless, but missed and so the huge stone fell into the river. Whether it's truth or fiction is unknown, but above the village in the mountains there formed a small lake, a lake known through the whole land of Eli for it's incredible trout. From early spring until late summer, Elish's father went to the mountain lake to fish. He sold the caught trout in the city during the Friday's bazaar.

By noon they had arrived. Unwrapping the horse's bridle, the father prepared the fishing gear, he gave the children their fishing rods and walked towards the shore. He swung the tip of the fishing rod towards the lake and sat down on a large smooth stone near the water's edge.

Elish's brother and sister also swung their little fishing rods towards the water. However, their lines were so messed up and twisted that it was impossible to fish for anything. They tried to unravel everything in frustration but they couldn't do it no matter how hard they tried.

"It's all your fault!" Shouted the sister and pulled the fishing rod fussily towards herself. "I told you to wait until I put the bait into the water first!"

"And what makes you think I'll listen to you." The little brother did not admit his mistake and also pulled his fishing rod to himself.

Father intervened and Elish breathed with relief. *"It's about time you did what you were told."* thought Elish, unable to bear the racket.

"Come on, calm down! You're scaring all the fish!" His father shouted irritably. "Is it really so hard to unravel the fishing lines?"

All three of them turned to Elish for help. But he looked the other way. The boy just spotted a beautiful willow on the other side of the lake. It's thin branches, gracefully curving, stretched to the watersedge, barely dipping beneath the dazzling blue surface.

"Elish, help your little brother and sister," asked his father.

Elish looked annoyingly at the fishing rods. "This really couldn't be easier - two lines and a dozen knots!" Elish judged. He was glad to be able to tear himself away from the monotonous fishing. A few skillful movements were enough to untangle the lines. The children, having received their fishing rods, fell silent, sat down on a stone beside their father and began to fish.

Elish, taking advantage of the fact that the rest are busy fishing, sneaked away quietly. And of course, he went to the willow. The boy neatly tore off a willow branch, sat onto the ground, and his hands, almost by themselves, bent it into a nice little knot, then another, and another …

Elish was so carried away by the weaving that he forgot both his father and his younger siblings. A little while later he had already made a basket made entirely of willow twigs. It was round, one and a half feet wide, with many small holes at the sides.

Only after finishing weaving the basket, Elish noticed that his father and siblings were waving their arms. Picking up his brand new creation, he wandered after them.

Seeing Elish's basket in his hands, his brother and sister pounced for it. The sister pulled it in one direction, the brother in another, and Elish in the third …

And so just before the basket could be broken the father's thunderous voice yelled furiously at the children. They were startled in fright and released the basket from their grasps. Elish let go a little later than his brother and sister and the basket was thrown over his head into the lake behind him.

The father's overwhelmed gaze pierced Elish.

"When are you ever going to do something serious? All you do every day is weave and weave, but what do you even learn? Go and do something useful for once. At least dig up the bait next time we go fishing!"

Uninvited Guest

The fish just weren't biting. For the whole day the family caught only a couple of small fry. The father sat hunched over, gloomy and silent.

Then at dawn, as the morning sun ascended above the horizon, there at the top of the hill, towering beyond the lake, a horseman appeared. The horse and it's rider approached the unlucky fishermen. The father passed his fishing rod to Elish and headed towards the stranger.

"Peace be upon you fellow peasant!" The horseman greeted him.

"And peace to you too, rider!" Answered the father.

"I see that you are fishing, it would be a pleasure to have dinner with a good carp or trout, and since yesterday i haven't eaten more than a slice of bread!" The rider took a small leather pouch out of his pocket and slipped out two silver coins.

"My noble horseman, I'm terribly sorry but I can not sell you fish. If you are hungry, you can come and dine with us from what I brought from home." The father said sadly and pointed to a pot of cooked broth.

"Did I offer too small a price?" Asked the rider.

"No, in fact the opposite, your price is very high. But I'm just not lucky. My catch is but a couple of small fry. I'm ashamed to offer them to a guest."

"Fellow peasant, never say that you are not lucky only because the fish don't bite. Luck can not be measured by the size of the fish caught. I'll dine with you from one pot, and then continue my journey!" The stranger placed the silver coins in the palm of the fathers hand.

The father looked down and felt embarrassed. *What to I do? I took supplies only for three days. And judging by the man's size, the guest's appetite is voracious! That and he'll probably end up eating everything! On the other hand, the traveler should not be denied food.* The peasant pondered.

"Sit by the fire, sir. I'll pour you some broth. But I will not take your money! I did not sell you fish and I will not take payment for the soup, as feeding a hungry traveler is the duty of any decent person. This is my condition." the father stated firmly and returned the coins to the stranger. Elish sneered under his breath, he could not understand why he would sell the fish for money but not the broth, what good does that do them.

"And you are clearly not without courage, an unarmed man, you demand a condition to another with a sword on his belt," the rider respected the nobility of the commoner.

"Courage has nothing to do with it. You're hungry, and I have food, there's your whole condition," the father muttered.

The horseman approached the lake, got off his horse and bent down to wash his face. He scooped up water in his hands and then suddenly burst out laughing

"Fellow peasant, why do you say you don't have fish when there are plenty?"

The rider reached into the water and pulled out ... a basket. Yes, the same one that Elish wove and which the children had lost in the lake. Two big trout wriggled in the basket. The father's face lit up as he whistled in surprise.

"Luck is with you my boy," the father said to his son, and turning to the stranger, continued: "This is my son. Always weaving things. He weaves something but we would always throw it away. Though this is a wondrous sight!"

Bridle

The fish that was cooked on the charcoal was eaten in just a couple of minutes and everyone was full and very satisfied. Then from the afternoon heat, everyone was feeling very sleepy. The two children could not resist the chance to relax, they lay down in the shade and fell asleep. Elish sat aside, pulled out a couple of twigs and begun to weave.

The rider gave the horse a drink and began to pack. After completing the preparations, he ran his hand over the worn out bridle, looking like it can tear at any minute, and said:

"Fellow peasant! I must certainly make my trip to 'The City-by-the-Sea' by Friday at noon. I'm afraid the bridle will not hold out for that long. Will you kindly sell me yours?"

"I would be delighted, but unfortunately my own horse is without a bridle." The father confessed.

"Perhaps you have a belt?"

"No, sir. I'm not even sure in what way I can assist you," the father spread his hands, apologising.

The rider closed his eyes and froze, then, tapping the ground with his right foot repeatedly, he pondered on an answer. And then, without opening his eyes, he said:

"Perhaps your son will help me out? Elish, correct?, will you be willing to tweak my bridle?"

Elish shrugged.

"And what exactly can you weave." Asked the rider.

"Any knots, for example, star-knots, spider-knots or my favorite, the back-tangled knot. It is very interesting. When you first weave it in, it's quite large, however it will then contract... " Elish could talk for hours about his favorite hobby.

"Good, good. As I can see, you know quite a lot about knots …" The guest interrupted.

Again, the boy shrugged his shoulders and thought: *Not only about knots, I can tell him about braids, and about loops ..."* An idea popped into his head and his face lit up, he ran towards the forest to look for strong and flexible branches. He returned with an armful of different twigs, he dropped them on the ground and laid them down to size - from the thickest to the thinnest

and he began to weave. The rider watched in amazement at how skillfully Elish handles the twigs.

When the bridle was ready, Elish handed it to the rider.

"I've never seen anything like it!" The rider admitted, admiringly examining the braid entwined within.

The rider gave his father two silver coins for the fish and two more gold for the bridle. He did not say goodbye, jumped on his horse and rode away. The father stood indecisively, holding silver coins in one hand, and in the other - gold.

He slowly weighted the coins, lifting his right hand, then his left. Then the father grinned and told the children to gather - the fishing was over. He never had such a generous catch. They collected everything, even the basket, and headed home. Elish was very happy, for the first time his father appreciated his enthusiasm for his hobby of weaving.

THE AMBASSADOR

PART TWO

In which the rider departs with gifts for the Dark Wizard.

The City-by-the-Sea

The 'City-by-the-Sea' stood on the shore of the Salt Sea, at the very end of an elongated hilly headland. The headland stretched for many miles into the rough dark waters.

The travellers called this place the Land of Fires, for the mysterious blue flames that burst from the dark depths of the earth. On the maps, the image of the headland resembled that of the head of an eagle, holding in its beak a precious pearl - the City-by-the-Sea.

The powerful fortress walls covered the city from the mainland with a broad arch. The ends of the stone arch stretch into the sea, far beyond the surf line.

Although the fortress walls did not cover the city from the sea, the entrance to its harbor was closed to foreign ships: the bottom of the bay was covered with thousands of underwater rocks which could sink any ship, however this pile of rocks had a hidden route through. Only the city's sailors could pilot through this dangerous labyrinth, who kept the path in the strictest of secrecy.

The city was built of white limestone, which was mined in state quarries on the headland. The fortress walls were erected from the debris of black sea cliffs. Because of the high walls, only the tall, slender and dark green cypresses could be seen from the other side.

They are like unreplaceable guards, lined up in two rows along the wall. All other greenery - fruit trees, canopies of roses, grapes and all sorts of flowers shyly hide behind the tall fortress walls.

A true reward for any traveller tired on the hot sandy road! Put yourself in the shoes of any man who wanders and wonders in the middle of a dying desert, trotting along the road that twists between the sandy dunes of the Land of Fires.

He can't possibly imagine the abundance of greenery in which the city is buried. And, finally, he gets inside the 'City-by-the-Sea' and he is greeted by the cool shade and fragrant scent of the city gardens.

The Minister

Along the raging sandy road, riding atop a black horse, the rider rode quickly. The clouds of dust that exploded into the air with every step, the same that raised the pacing horse, were noticed from afar by the guard in the keep inside the fortress walls. The senior guard tightened his belt, adjusted the helmet on his head and went out of the gate, towards the rider.

Not long ago were peaceful times, where the city gates were opened day and night, but in the last couple of months came disturbing news from the north. Some merchants who returned from there said that the Dark Wizard poisoned the king, took his daughter as his wife and took the kingdoms throne.

Others claimed that the northern tribes themselves overthrew the king and elected the Dark Wizard as the ruler. There were rumors that the Dark Wizard was gathering a large army, but no one knew who he wanted to declare war on. The Khan of the 'City-by-the-Sea' ordered to disarm all men carrying weapons at the entrance of the city.

Approaching the city gates, the traveler held his horse back. The senior guard gestured the rider to stop:

"Entrance to the city with a sword in possession is prohibited!"

The horseman pulled down the cloth that covered his face and said:

"Peace be with you Keshish! But please, I can not be delayed, for I must see the ruler as soon as possible."

The guard recognized the younger son of the minister.

"And peace to you too! Forgive me, Vashag, for I had not recognized you. I dare not detain you. But on the way to the Shah's palace, go to the hamam. You're covered in dust and dirt from head to toe and it would be a good idea to clean up.

Otherwise you will soon be mistaken for a drifter, than for the son of the minister!"

Smiling, the rider spurred his horse and rushed through the narrow streets of the city directly to the Shah's palace.

The Shah's Palace

The residents of the city were fleeing from the burning sun in the shady courtyards behind high fences. Running through half-empty streets Vashag quickly reached the Shah's palace. Standing in the plaza in front of the palace, he stopped to admire the majestic building.

Twelve centuries ago, the great Shah Kay Qaboos the Second ordered the construction of a palace, equal to no other that exists on the whole coast of the Salt Sea. The sacred hill near the northern fortress wall of the 'City-by-the-Sea' was chosen as the place for the palace.

Construction was hard and long: there was not enough money in the treasury, then hunger and disease wiped out most of the workers. The proud Shah Kay Qaboos the Second died without seeing his palace completed. The construction was finally finished by his great-grandson Shah Kay Qaboos the Fourth.

Disputes about whether the luxurious palace cost those victims, the labor, the lives of those unfortunate slaves, do not cease to this day. However, hardly anyone will doubt its external magnificence and richness of its interior decoration. The palace was so beautiful that the superstitious Shah surrounded it with a high wall - away from the mischievous eyes and envious looks.

The Shah's dynasty had existed for many generations as rulers of the 'City-by-the-Sea' and the Land of Fires. However over the years, the Shah's became less and less interested in what was happening outside their palace walls.

And thus the city fell into decay, and the Shah's palace, on the contrary, became more and more drowned in luxury. The last seven generations of the Shah dynasty ruled the 'City-by-the-Sea' without leaving the palace even once. They had forgotten how sand looks, because they walked only on the marble floors of their chambers.

They had forgotten the salty taste of seawater, because they only drank water from the silver bowls and golden fountains. And when a big war broke out, Shah Kay Qaboos the Fifteenth locked himself in the impenetrable citadel of his palace, as if the war, like a harsh winter, would just pass by itself.

Fortunately among the inhabitants of the city were brave individuals. A commoner named Ashina led the people behind him. The 'City-by-the-Sea' lost the war and lost its possessions in the south and in the north, but found a new ruler - Ashina the Khan.

And so the dynasty of the Shah's, of the 'City-by-the-Sea' went down in history. The dynasty was gone, and the Shah's palace remained. What happened to Shah Kay Qaboos the Fifteenth is unknown. Nobody wanted to open the doors of the citadel in the Shah's palace. But even now, during the darkest of nights, from behind the locked citadel doors, the lone laugh of the Shah is heard echoing through the palace walls.

Since those events had passed two centuries ago the Khans were elected as lifelong rulers by the Kurultai, the ones who ruled the 'City-by-the-Sea'. Chosen by the warriors of the city and only from a number of soldiers. The Khans were forbidden to have heirs, and if their sons were born, upon reaching adulthood they were sent to seek death in the fields of battle.

By the order of the Khans, a spacious tent was pitched in the courtyard. The tent was so large that a small fountain and a pool with goldfish fits inside it.

The water gurgled peacefully, pouring from a gilded fountain into a snow-white marble basin. The Khan stood by the pool and watched the fish. Hearing the footsteps behind him, he gradually, as befits a true ruler, turned and saw the minister's son and smiled broadly.

"Peace be upon you, great Khan!"

"Hello Vashag. You were gone for a long time. Your father's soul was devoured by the fears for the fate of his heir."

"I'm sure the ruler did not fail to take care of his minister. Though I must admit I haven't visited home yet. I had decided above all else to deliver the ruler the news from the north.

"You must have brought me an important messages if you put the duty of delivery above the respect of your elders." The Khan suggested.

"My father always taught me how to place respect on one side of the scale, and on the other the official duty and weigh it. And then follow the one that turned out to be heavier."

The Khan always dreamed of such a son that will not be his heir. But God had only given him daughters.

"Great Khan, I've brought disturbing news. The northerners have submitted to the Dark Wizard. They say that he poisoned their king and now reigns as his black heart desires. Many northerners swore allegiance to him, some refused and were exiled, and the rest live in fear. Great Khan, the north has changed a lot. The laws of the Dark Wizard are severe, punishments are cruel, and his intentions are clouded in mystery.

"All the worse for the northern lands. The farmer must go out into the field because he loves the land, and not out of fear of his ruler. From fear ones harvest will not be any greater," argued the Khan. "But something more serious is tormenting you isn't it, since you've called it disturbing."

"Northern cities are covered with soot and coal, in forges blacksmiths work day and night. Over the cities black clouds gather, and soon they will burst with lightning." Vashag warned seriously as he pierced the rulers gaze.

"Do you think there's a war coming?" The Khan stared into Vashag's eyes.

"I can't say for sure. I stayed in the northern lands for a very short time, and it's not exactly easy to enter the palace of the northern kingdom."

"Rest for three days, then collect a dozen warriors and go north as my ambassador. We do not need war, but we are not afraid to raise our swords either. And if war is what is destined to be, it is necessary to know about it in advance.

The Khan emerged from the cool shadow of the tent and saw the dark clouds rumbling quietly in the north.

"This hot summer will soon become a freezing winter." He said thoughtfully.

A Dozen

The son of the minister called eleven of his comrades with him - all of them were warriors who've fought in battle. The troops gathered early in the morning in the courtyard of the Shah's palace. Warriors riding horses lined up against the wall opposite the gate, opening onto the market square.

To their right was a stone staircase that rose to a heavy oak door. The door was covered with a fine carving with the coat of arms with the Khan in the center. Above the door, a calligraphy carved on the gray stone said:

One life for a dozen - heroism.
A dozen lives for thousands - glory.
Thousands of lifes for one - love.

Vashag stood at the stairs. His face was calm and focused. For once the minister's son was looking at the inscription above the door. But only now it seemed that he understood the true meaning of the words hidden in the ligature of the quaint patterns.

The door opened and the Khan came out into the courtyard, followed by the ministers and two of the Khan's advisers.

"Khan sag olsun!" Vashag said the traditional greeting, and eleven soldiers echoed behind him.

The Khan descended down a couple steps and stopped:

"You have a dangerous path ahead of you. The northerners are no different when it comes to hospitality, and they do not offend travelers in vain. Is it so now? I do not know. However, the dangers that await in the future, will be balanced with the wisdom of your leader.

"If you sacrifice your life and save a dozen - you're a hero!" The first part of the calligraphy has always been close in spirit to Vashag.

The Khan put his right hand on Vashags shoulder as a father would. Vashag glanced into the Khan's eyes. Saying anything was unnecessary, they understood each other without any words.

"And if a dozen, after sacrificing themselves, save thousands - their legend will be remembered with great glory!" Vashag repeated the second part of the calligraphy to himself.

The advisor took a wide ribbon out of a leather bag and handed it over to Vashag. The ribbon was green, with a gold coat of arms at the end. A peace treaty was beautifully inscribed as calligraphy on the ribbon.

According to the tradition of Eli, all the oaths were recorded on ribbons, which were tied on the sacred Tree of Oaths.

"Bring the Dark Wizard our offer of peace and back it up with generous gifts." The Khan said, handing the ribbon to Vashag.

Laying the ribbon in a saddlebag, Vashag once again checked the harness on the black horse. The Khan, as an experienced rider, immediately noticed the unusual bridle. At other times he would have questioned Vashag about it, but at that moment he considered it an inappropriate moment to ask.

Vashag jumped into the saddle and, spurring his horse, trotted out of the gate. Eleven soldiers raced off behind their leader. The Khan, in deep thought, climbed the stairs and returned to the palace. The advisers followed him. The minister did not take his eyes off the road for a long time, his son moving farther and farther away, unaware of the dangers that await him.

Iron Gate

The merchant caravans take around three months to overcome the path from the 'City-by-the-Sea' to the northern lands. A troop of twelve soldiers was to get to the Dark Lord in a month. Otherwise, they will not have time to return to the 'City-by-the-Sea' before the winter frosts come and deep snow blocks the narrow roads.

In the north, the border of the Khan's territory reached the place that they called the isthmus, a natural stone bridge that connected either ends. Here the spurs of Mount Kaf approached the shore of the Salt Sea so close, that at the foot of the mountain, one could hear the waves crashing down below. A thousand years ago, the righteous ruler ordered the erection of a fortress whose walls would block the passage through the narrow isthmus from Mount Kaf to the Salt Sea. The fortress was called the Iron Gate.

Vashag's troop took less than a week to reach the Iron Gates. The fortress was the last outpost - behind it the power of the Khan came to an end and with it, order and law. The places behind the Gate were dangerous, and the farther from the Iron Gate, the more dangerous they became.

There was a small garrison in the fortress. At the head of the garrison was Vashag's elder brother - Babir. The fortress gates open and Babir stepped out to greet the troop.

"And here I thought my younger brother will never leave the cozy capital. Everyone there sits on silk feather-beds, and he became so used to it's soothing luxury that he forgot how to ride the sturdy saddle." Babir loved to make fun of Vashag since childhood.

"Do not worry big brother, I took my favorite silk feather beds for the road!" Retorted Vashag.

The brothers laughed and hugged each other tightly.

"We'll spend the night in the fortress, and tomorrow we'll continue our journey." Vashag ordered.

The brothers have not seen each other for a long time - they had so much to tell one another. They retired to the fortress' citadel. Babir's room was located at the very top of the highest tower. Its windows opened to the south - the calm lands of the Khan, and to the north - the source of alarm for the garrison of the fortress.

"So, little brother, what brought you here? Did the Khan send you for a swap over with me at the outpost?"

"I'd love to stay here instead of you, would be nice if you went north to the Dark Lord instead of me!"

"You're not kidding are you Vashag? Traveling on the northern roads is very dangerous. Your troop is too small to defeat gangs of bandits that prey on travellers, and is too large to pass unnoticed by the Dark Lord's spies.

Alright, how about this! You stay here, and I'll go instead of you. I'm an experienced pathfinder, I've been to the north many times, I know all the secret roads. After I return from the north to the Iron Gate, you will go to the Khan and tell him everything."

"No. You should stay here and I'll carry on my journey to the north. This is the order of the ruler."

"The Khan will never know if I'll go north instead of you."

"Stop it Babir. The rulers order will not be debated. The Khan knows of your abilities. But he has also heard of your temper. He made a decision, and we must obey. How about we eat! I hope you'll be generous and fry a nice juicy lamb for us?"

Arguing loudly, the brothers went down into the hall, where the rest of the warriors waited for them. After eating supper, they went to bed early. The troop rose at dawn. Babir packed the soldiers with supplies from the reserves of the fortress. The new supply bags, hammered to the brim, burdened the sides of spare packhorses.

As Vashag turned to say goodbye, Babir held out a cage with a dove inside in front of him:

"It's a magic bird. Wherever you are, whisper my name to her, and she will fly to me. Any three words you say before, she will remember and repeat into my ear. So I'll find out if you get into trouble."

"It will be hard for me to take care of her on the way. I'm afraid the bird will suffer the northern colds. Better to leave her here." Vashag said, and jumped into the saddle.

"This is my best postal dove Vashag. She always finds her way home. So if the little bird will burden a dozen healthy warriors, just let her go and she'll come back to me."

"Time goes by, and yet your love for those birds never changes."

"Here, at the edge of the world, it's the only kind of entertainment you can get." Babir said, taking Vashag's horse by the bridle.

Babir looked at the braided bridle with bewilderment. He squeezed it in his fist, doubting its strength.

"You have a strange harness, brother." Babir looked up at Vashag.

"The harness is ordinary. Only the bridle is special. A gift from an unusual boy."

"Watch out, the northerners might laugh at you."

"Laughter is the best language for an ambassador ..." Vashag turned his horse and rode away.

THE INSIDIOUS WIZARD

PART THREE

In which Vashag is captured by the Dark Wizard

The Crossing

At the end of the fortieth day, Vashag's troop reached the town of Itil, the capital of the Dark Lord. Having passed the guards at the gate, the troop entered the city. Vashag decided to walk along the main street directly to the royal palace, as befits the ambassador of the great Khan.

There were few passers-by on the streets, and there were no children at all. In order to not draw attention to their foreign language, the soldiers remained silent. Deprived of the opportunity to speak, they felt under pressure.

They were tired. A long transition through boundless steppes, open spaces and dense forests will greatly exhaust anyone. But even compared to them, the faces of the people in the city of Itil were a lot more gloomy and lifeless.

The main street of Itil has always been the focus of fun and joy. Here artists and musicians from all over the north flocked. They set up near benches and shops, exposing their creations on the street. Life on the main street used to boil, but now it is empty. Many houses were boarded up. And those in which people still lived, were tightly locked.

"I can't recognize this place. Before, people here were so cheerful and carefree, but now all I see around me are sullen and angry expressions!" Exclaimed one of the twelve warriors, unable to bear the pressure of the blank, staring faces.

"Yes, the city is not the same as it was before. This street was full of shops with artists, paintings and carvings. But now only their black shadow remains on the street, black from the forge's soot!" Another echoed him.

"And because of this Itil is now called the Black City. And now be quite. Not a word more!" Ordered Vashag.

Dark Wizard

The Dark Lord was informed that the ambassador arriving from the 'City-by-the-Sea' asked him for an audience. When the twelve soldiers appeared before the newly-made king of the north, he built up a displeased face and muttered irritatedly.

Many neighboring kingdoms - kings and princes have already expressed to him their location and obedience. But the proud Khan of the 'City-by-the-Sea' was not about to bow his head to this powerful sorcerer. The Dark Lord considered the Khan's love of freedom an irresponsible impudence and was determined to punish the obstinate ruler!

Vashag read his expressions in complete rage, and even the Dark Lord himself did not particularly hide his treacherous intentions.

"Please don't waste your breath! For I am only the ambassador of the Khan of the 'City-by-the-Sea,' an idle man and a scapegrace. I've brought the ribbon with the treaty of eternal peace. We are skilled masons, whom the Khan sent to build a bridge as a sign of the peace between us ..." Vashag spoke quickly, so that only his men could hear these words. Vashag breathed in and then out, he stepped forward and quietly but yet clearly said:

"Peace be with you great ruler!"

The Dark Wizard responded in his native tongue, gibberish to the soldiers before him. The wizard could easily speak the same language, but he deliberately spoke in his own way and waited arrogantly until the servants translated his words. Showing disrespect to those who came as guests with the gift of peace.

"And if peace is with me then how about you? Hope you didn't leave yours just lying about." The servant translated his words.

The warriors exchanged glances at the frankly unfriendly response of the Dark Wizard. The black intentions of the sorcerer became obvious to them then. However, Vashag ignored the wizards remark and calmly continued:

"Of course, we came in peace. And with gifts from our ruler. The great Khan sent skillful masons. As a sign of the friendship between us, they will erect a stone bridge where ever you desire."

The Dark Wizard narrowed his eyes, making his face seem even more cunning.

"Well, then I must accept with honour, according to the high ranking envoys of the great Khan. You are to be taken to the hall, where we will dine together." The servant translated.

The group of twelve followed the mischievous servants into a large black castle that loomed over them as if a beast about to devour its prey.

Dark corridors led them to a large half-empty room. Hanging on the wall were curtained paintings that were as black as the wizard's heart. Over the broken stained glass, the crooked bars stood, rooted into the building's foundation. In the middle of the hall stood a long iron table and twelve chairs.

The Dark Wizard and his retinue occupied a table that stood at a distance from the iron one, one that stood atop a raised platform. When the food was brought, Vashag, following his traditional ways, thanked the host for the warm welcome. The sorcerer said nothing. Instead of him, a man with an horrific scarred face appeared from behind the table. He walked into the center of the room and drew a large circle on the floor with a piece of chalk

"What a strange custom?" Asked Yalov, the youngest of Vashag's troop.

"It's not a custom Yalov. The Dark Lord wants us to know that the whole world belongs to him," said Vashag, discreetly in disgust. Then he got up, thanked the host again, went up to the circle and drew a line with the chalk that crossed it in two equal halves.

"You get your half and we get ours." Vashag said returning to the table and then beginning to eat..

However, the other table did not stop there. Less than a quarter of an hour, another warrior from the master's table went into the center of the hall. He drew his sword from its scabbard and threw it into the center of the circle.

"It appears that we have no other choice." Vashag warned his comrades and rose from the table.

Vashag stood at the edge of the circle and threw his round shield in to it so that it covered the sword. Above the shield he put the green ribbon of the oath of peace, which the Khan had offered .

Before Vashag could rejoin his comrades, the Dark Wizard said something in a language that everyone understood:

"Unfortunately you are too blind to see the power I possess as ruler of these lands. All around your great Khan there are many insightful people who very clearly understand 'who' should be ruler of this world.

In fact some of them can see more clearly with one eye than you with two. And yet the Khan sent me this buffoon, and not one who is more compliant!" The sorcerer straightened to his full height and lifting his staff over his head, continued. "Messenger, your message is clear to me. I need to consider how to respond to the Khan. In the meantime, I think you'll have to wait."

The sorcerer signaled to the guard, and he, exposing his sword, surrounded Vashag and his men in a crowded ring. Vashag was about to pull out his sword but he knew resistance was futile. There are thousands of slaves under the Dark Lord that surround the castle - twelve swords will blunt too soon before his dark army would run out of men to fight them. Vashag made the decision to not shed his people's blood.

He ordered his soldiers to give their swords to the guard. Yalov was disarmed last, he who did not want to part with his blade.

Vashag's men were grabbed and dragged out one by one. A huge, heavy man got a thick rope and tied a tight noose.

"Well, who here is in charge?" He mumbled.

"Me!" Vashag proudly said without hesitation.

The huge man threw a noose around Vasang's neck and, wrapping the other end around his arm, pulled it towards himself. But Vashag slid his foot into the gap between the stone slab and leaning back with all his strength, pulled the rope.

His comrades started to cheer for their captain but then the other guards jumped down and twisted Vashag's foot from between the slabs.

The huge man, breathing heavily, rose from the ground. His eyes filled with blood. From anger, he tightened the rope around his neck so tight that it became difficult for him to breathe. From the same rope, the man tied another loop and threw it around the neck of another warrior. This time two guards held onto the prisoner and held them tightly. And so one warrior after another were trapped by their nooses, all tied up to one long rope.

The captured warriors were led to the farmyard. The very same one where they had just unpacked their supplies. The horses were taken to the royal stables. That's of course with the exception of Vashag's, no one could cope with it - the stubborn animal did not let anyone in, it kicked and bitt.

The fat boss of the guards, all smeared with mud with his earlier encounter with the horse, snarled at Vashag:

"Your horse is just like you! Ill-mannered as you are! I noticed it when you drove into town, a fine horse. Calm him, or else he won't let me into the saddle. Do it and I'll loosen the rope on your neck just a little, I'll admit our 'giant' overdid it by just a bit.

It hurt to part with the horse. Vashag took the horse by the bridle and whispered something. The horse calmed down and stood still. The cheerful chief jumped into the saddle and snatched the bridle from Vashag's hand.

Even touching the beautifully braided bridle caused a great discomfort for the Chief.

"A bridle like this really says alot about a man as proud as you, though the harness is more like a poor man's!" The fat chief removed the bridle and threw it to Vashag. "We are honest people, we do not need someone else's!"

Under the foolish laughter of the guards, the 'giant' tied a noose from the bridle and threw it around Vashag's neck.

The Mountain

The captives were sent far north. A place where there were no villages, no cities, where among the deserted forest thickets was the dungeon of the Dark Lord. In the cave below the mountain he kept his captives imprisoned. A cave that was larger than any city.

It was a huge maze with thousands of tunnels and rooms, large halls and low niches. A damp, dark, deep and gloomy prison, a prison that seemed almost endless. There were rumors that the Dark Wizard was once imprisoned in the cave, the sorcerer spent hundreds of years trapped underneath the mountain. And now that he was out, the sorcerer exiles all those who do not like him to the very same cave that once held his dark soul away from the light of the surface.

The prisoners went to the foot of the Mountain. The road along the dreary canyon went up steeply and led to an unpassable cliff-edge. All the trees in the forest were mercilessly squished together, and along the road they were knocked over and covered with mud, as if a terrible storm had swept over them.

Vashag and his detachment were not the only prisoners. Several northerners were tied up to their rope in the city. As the caravan of bound people moved farther north, more and more prisoners were added to it. Vashag went ahead, followed by eleven soldiers, followed by a dozen northerners.

"Vashag, except for us, none of the captives are familiar with a sword! It seems that the Dark Lord drives down all the craftsmen and masters into the caves. What kind of danger do they pose?" Yalov whispered to Vashag.

"We shouldn't have said that we were masons..." another warrior added.

"The Dark Wizard hates everyone that does not serve him. He does not need a master of colored stained glass or a master of painting? He only needs swords, well, and blacksmiths to forge these swords." said Vashag

"Hush! Come already!" The escort barked..

The warriors were engulfed by the darkness of the cave and were instantly overwhelmed by it's magnitude.

"Yea-ah... I've never seen an dungeon such as this," said one warrior. "They don't even need bars, nor chains. Even locks and shackles won't change anything."

"I found something hopeful! You see the sun peeks through the dungeon at a certain time of the day, but then it goes and you're covered in the darkest of black once again!" Sighed Yalov.

The passage that led to the entrance of the cave was three to four people tall. On each side were two cliffs, carved into columns; and then one more rock, like a crossbeam, lay on top of them. Above the entrance, on the crossbar, in the rock was broken some inscription. Vashag understood the language of the northerners, but could not read them.

"Your food should be earned: 'gather up ore, and food you'll get more!'" Said the elderly guard of the cave and pointed his bony finger at the inscription above the entrance.

The escorts were eager to return to the Black City:

"Let's get the supplies!"

One of the guards of the cave made a sour face, but still got up and went to the captives. He cut rope that connected Vashag with the rest of the captives with a sword. Two other guards, taking Vashag by the shoulders, led him to the edge of the cliff, where he could see the prisoners working under his feet.

"Do not yell loudly, or you'll wake up the bats above us, they won't let us rest until the morning comes!" The guard said, then pushed Vashag deep into the cave, into the dark below.

Vashag felt himself fall. In the dark nothing was visible. Of course, he cried out, although later he did not admit it. His cry was still echoing through the gorge, as the next prisoner, and then the third and all the others, were thrown down behind him.

WHICKERWORK

PART FOUR

In which Elish is invited to a feast with the great Khan

Wickerwork

From the severe northern thickets we return to our hero.

After meeting with Vashag, Elish's life changed a little. He still spent all his free time in the barn, all alone. Although after the story with the fish caught in the basket, others began to notice that his weaving had some benefit.

Once the father asked Elish whether he could weave a chair for him. "Of course!" Answered the boy. However, wishing to show his father his skill, Elish wove too many 'flowers' in the back of the chair, 'flowers' were some of Elish's most complex patterns.

My father considered the chair childish and gave it to Elish's little sister. His father did not ask more of him after that. Also his sister once asked him to weave a doll - Elish could not refuse her. The doll turned out beautiful, almost like the real deal.

"Elish! Stop playing around with your twigs already!" The children from the street called for him.

"It's not a game! It's important! It's necessary for …" Elish faltered.

"Who needs you're little woven nick-nacks?! Let's go play!"

"This is for the rider!" Elish did not know anyone except the rider who would find his hobby useful.

To increase his knowledge, Elish pretended that he actually wanted to go with his father on the Friday's bazaar.

All day Elish went with his father between stalls that barted with horns and hoofs in order to get a minute and run off to look at the harness of the Khan's warriors horses . While the riders explored the weapon shops, Elish examined their horses.

He tried to keep every detail in his memory. Details that were difficult to remember, he hastily wove from the scraps of an old rope.

Returning to the village, Elish began to work. The boy did not show anyone what he was weaving. Elish feared that if his father saw that he was weaving a horse harness, he would decide that his son wanted to run away from home. However for Elish this was further from the truth, he always felt the utter horror of the thought that he would someday have to leave his native village.

Elish would sometimes wonder why and for whom he weaves the bridles and knots, braids and nooses, because the answer to that question, he himself did not know.

The Best Harness

We all know very well that in fairy tales and in life nothing happens just like that. Everything has its own purpose. Sometimes major events seem to be caused by random accidents. However, later, having looked more closely, one can notice how one event entails another, or even that, unconnected events take on an explicit link and weave into a single chain.

And so, at the very same time as Elish's actions took place, the Khan of the 'City-by-the-Sea' announced that after the harvest, he would arrange a festival. On the third day of this holiday, townspeople and visitors will compete to make the best horse harness. The one, whose harness will be recognized as the most beautiful, is promised a horse from royal stables of the Khan himself and beautifully woven festive pouch, with one pocket that will be filled with gold and the other with silver.

And by chance that on the very day when the herald of the Khan appeared in the village of Gyrusly and announced the competition that will take place at the 'City-by-the-Sea', the father looked into the barn for Elish but instead discovered a horse harness lying on the ground.

The father sat down in surprise. He looked at the miracle that his son wove. The first thought was to take the harness to the 'City-by-the-Sea' and take part in the match. The father picked up the harness to better examine the work of Elish. The harness was in fact incredibly beautiful.

Different twigs and bindweeds intertwined in bizarre combinations that resembled a rich carpet with many small patterns. On the other hand, it was completely different from the usual battle harness and the father was afraid that they would be laughed at.

However, the reward promised by the Khan was so generous that he decided to try his luck. Elish did not object or argue. After he was finished he had no further interest in it. And when it came to giving his harness away, he agreed at once but resisted the trip to the 'City-by-the-Sea': he was frightened by meeting dozens of strangers in an unfamiliar city.

Father was adamant and insisted on the trip. He believed that if the Khan chooses their harness, then Elish must be present at the time.

The next morning the father prepared a waggon. He carefully folded the harness into a bag of rough fabric and covered with a leather cape. The father climbed into the wagon, Elish settled next to him. The weather in the mountains began to darken.

Heavy rain clouds swarmed the sky. Elish wrapped himself in a cloak. He loved autumn and winter because when it was cold and rainy outside he did not need to explain why he didn't want to leave the house.

The father pulled on the reins and the wagon began to move. Suddenly, Elish's younger sister jumped out from the leather cape under which her father had covered the harness. In her hands she held a doll, woven by her brother.

"Take her with you! If you're ever sad, you can talk to her and you will feel better!" She handed the doll to Elish.

Trying to explain to his sister that he does not need to talk with a doll was meaningless. The stubborn little girl will still force him to take it. "I'll give it back when I return." Thought Elish and put the doll inside his bag.

Big City - Little Man

When Ilish and his father finally crossed the desert they reached the 'City-by-the-Sea', the festivities were in full swing. A competition that they had sought after was scheduled for the next day. The competition for the best horse harness.

The father and son did not have any relatives in the 'City-by-the-Sea', thus they had to stay over in a travellers tavern. The doorkeeper of the tavern, a man in a black hat, a black mustache and black eyebrows opened the door and asked suspiciously:

"Who are ya?" The man had a funny twist to every word he said.

"We are from the village of Gyrusly, an place in the valley that holds the river Velvel, we came to participate in the harness competition tomorrow."

The doorkeeper looked at the father and then at his son and, softening a bit, said:

"Sorry bout that, before the fair, a lotta people came. And wherever there are many people, there are also many thieves and crooks, they go around stealing everyones things! There ain't no empty rooms in the caravan: all a them busy. But there is a big hall. Two families are staying in there, but there is plenty of room for y'all."

The father was very happy and immediately agreed. Moreover, they didn't have enough money for a separate room. The doorkeeper led them through a courtyard, and then down the narrow corridor to the hall.

The doorkeeper wasn't lying - the hall was really big and spacious. It was divided into several parts by wooden frames. There were no windows in the hall, it was lit by two oil lamps. The room was cool and very damp and incredibly quiet - you can barely hear the buzzling street outside, and even then only when the door opened.

The father laid a mat on the floor, a bedding and two pillows.

"Go to bed son. Tomorrow morning we'll wear your harness on our old horse."

And with that they both fell asleep soundly.

The City Centre

With the first rays of the sun the city came to life. Merchants opened their stalls, fresh bread was smelled from bakeries, hooves trotted over the stone pavement.

On the crooked narrow streets, the father and son headed towards square in front of the Shah's palace, where the match was supposed to be held. There were many people, as if everyone all across Eli gathered in the city centre of the 'City-by-the-Sea'.

On the square there was a festive performance: ropes stretched high in the air, where rope walkers would cross dangerously; next to them fought wrestlers who were undressed to the waist and rubbed with oil. There were also different magicians and one sorcerer in a long blue robe - they turned things into animals and back, made things disappear and reappear.

Of course, some of them were only frauds who shamelessly claimed to be real magicians, but the rest were skilled wizards.

From last night, the traders of dried fruits and spices set up pens for their horses. Father hurried to the nearest unoccupied pen. The entrance to the pen was blocked by a man with a magnificent grey beard, in light armor and with an axe in his hands. After asking them about who they were and where they came from he allowed them to get the horse into an empty paddock.

His father pulled down the veil revealing the saddle. Seeing it, woven from twigs and bindweeds, the old soldier was so surprised that he nearly let go of the axe. He grabbed the saddle and jerked it hard several times, checking it for strength. The saddle was very strong. The soldier nodded approvingly and went to another paddock, where a beautiful horse was stood with a scarlet harness richly trimmed with silver.

The Contest

The sounds of the trumpets were heard and cheering cries echoed through the city streets. The Khan and his retinue left the palace to take part in the festival. They crossed the square and approached the first pen. The Khan himself, as the herald assured, personally checked the work of each master, choosing the best harness. He proudly jumped into the saddle to try out the harness of the first master.

The horse stood on its hind legs and neighed, but the khan reassured the animal, patting it on the neck. "Good work, master!" The Khan was pleased with the harness. He jumped to the ground and headed for the second pen.

The Khan moved from one pen to another and compared the work of the masters. With some he lingered and talked with the masters for a long time, in others he stopped only out of politeness, not wanting to offend the guest.

The father did not take his eyes off the the Khan. "The Khan does is swayed by gold and silver, which the harness not far from theirs was trimmed with. He is only interested in the skill of the craftsman! " Concluded his father. Elish wasn't listening to him, he was watching with devotion as a woman weaved a carpet in the workshop opposite to their pen.

Finally came the turn for Elish and his father to be judged. The Khan shook hands with the father and said:

"Well, craftsman, show me your work!"

The father led the horse out of the pen. The Khan studied the harness in silence. He then looked at it closely, then walked a couple of steps and admired the harness at a distance. The retinue also kept silence.

"Can I try it?" Asked the Khan, not believing that the harness was sturdy.

"It will be an honour, great Khan!" Answered the father.

The Khan jumped into the saddle. At first he held tight and sat in the saddle uncertainty, still doubting its strength. But then he spurred the horse and galloped down the very street where Elish and his father came to the square. The Khan returned from the other side of the square.

People looked at the ruler in confusion: either because of the old horse under him, or because of the unusual harness.

"Is this your work" The Khan asked, dismounting.

"My son's," his father winked at Elish.

"In the evening I will have a feast in the palace. Your son is invited and you along with him!" The Khan patted Elish on the shoulder and went to the arena, with the crowd of wrestlers waiting patiently, where the winner was about to be decided.

"Congratulations." Said the minister. "In the evening we will be waiting for you in the Shah's palace."

The father could not believe that they won the competition, but the peasant did not dare to go back on the offer.

The Feast

Earlier that day, in the morning, two dozen cooks prepared the meals for Khan's guests. When the guests gathered in front of the Shah's palace, the chief cook walked between the tables and at the very last moment, made sure that the tables were covered impeccably and allowed the doors to be opened.

Seven long tables spread across the extended hall. The hall itself resembled a noisy hive: the guests slowly seated themselves, they chose places near familiar faces, then they moved closer to their friends, met their old comrades and again changed the table where they were called to by distant relatives, and they joined them. All these messy movements between the tables really put a strain on Elish.

In the far corner of the hall, the invited magicians were preparing to begin their performance, but due to the fact that many of the guests were still on their feet, Elish could not see them and it made him angrier than he already was.

The throne of the Khan was empty. In fact the Khan moved from one table to another. Every time he approached a new table, the guests rose to their feet, greeting the Khan, then they all sat down together and continued their meal. the Khan would then politely said goodbye to them and go on to the next table.

An hour later the feast was already in full swing: the guests were talking passionately, the musicians filled the room with wondrous music and the mages from ancient temples showed their knowledge of witchcraft and spells. The Khan said goodbye to the guests at their table, wishing them a safe return to their lands and went to the table where Elish and his father were sitting.

It so happened that the guest who was sitting to the right of Elish, seeing that at the next table his distant relative, a cousin from the northern slopes of Mount Kaf, was waving to him. The man left the chair and the place next to Elish was freed.

The Khan took the vacant seat and greeted the guests sitting at the table:

"Welcome. Eat, drink, enjoy this evening!"

The Khan did not have time to finish the greeting, as he was served a dish of pilaf, seasoned with chestnuts, raisins and fried meat.

"My fifth dish!" Said the Khan and everyone at the table laughed.

"He needs two more tables to get around. So he has two more plates to eat. Oh, it's not easy being a Khan! " Elish sympathized with the ruler

The Khan began to eat, as if it were the first table and the first dish. He managed to eat, and cope with the guests at the same time, who they were and where they came from, what news was brought from the distant lands of Eli and how the affairs of other Khans are going.

Finishing the pilaf, The Khan turned to the right: there was a tall and lean man with a pointy nose and a thick black beard. The Khan exchanged a few words with him and turned to the left. But there was nobody on the left! Khan bent his head down and noticed Elish. Either the table was high, or the chair was too low, but the boy's head barely reached the edge of the table.

So Elish put the plate on his knees and bending over it, ate his grilled fish with an appetite. The conversation at the table was quiet: everyone looked at the Khan, and he looked down at Elish with a smile. The boy felt that everyone's eyes where on him, and he didn't like it one bit!

"So this is our craftsman! What is your name, great master?" Asked the Khan; there was no tone of mockery in his voice.

"I only saw this kind of work once in my life. A bridle with a similar style was on the horse of Vashag, the son of the minister and a fellow rider of ours. Do you know who wove that bridle?"

The Khan smiled discreetly as if he knew exactly who had made it.

"The rider?" Elish's eyes lit up. "His bridle was worn out, and he asked me to help him. I did not have much time to prepare the twigs for the weaving; Hastily I searched the nearest forest for twigs and a couple of bindweeds. I was afraid my bridle would fail him on his journey."

"Well I'm happy to tell you that he got to the 'City-by-the-Sea' safely. He did not even change his bridle when he went on a dangerous journey to the north."

One of the guests intervened in the conversation:

"Great Khan, they've already harvested the crops, yet the ambassador has not returned from the northern lands."

"Yes, it's about time. Vashag is an experienced warrior and a cunning leader. He will not disappear and he will never put his men in danger." The Khan replied confidently.

However, his heart was heavy; Two days ago he had talked with the minister about Vashag and his troop. The ambassadors had long been due to arrive in the 'City-by-the-Sea'.

The oak door, covered with wrought bronze, suddenly opened and three armored men entered the room. The uninvited guests who stood in the middle of the hall, not joining any of the tables, clearly did not intend to take part in the feast.

They looked around, trying to find the Khan among hundreds of guests. The one that stood in the middle was holding something in his hands ... the very bridle that Elish had woven for the rider. The one known as Vashag, son of the minister.

PART FIVE

In which the dove carries away Elish's braided bridle

Footsteps in the Dark

The shaft that led to the entrance of the cave blocked the sunlight. Only a faint glimmer that seeped from above barely illuminated just a small section in the middle of the room; The darkness hid the walls and corners of the room. Vashag could not see his men: in the thick black one could only distinguish the vague outlines of other prisoners.

"It's impossible to climb the mine! The cliff face is too steep. Let's try to find another way!" Vashag said determined, without the slightest thought of giving up.

As if playing blind man's bluff, twelve adult men, putting their hands in front of them, felt around to find a way out of the room.

"Vashag, there's a way over here!" One of the soldiers found a corridor leading downwards.

"Let's see where this way leads us. Go whilst holding a string, otherwise we will lose someone in the darkness." Vashag ordered.

Gradually the group moved down the corridor. They walked in complete darkness.

"Ay!" There was a shout followed by a loud roar.

One of the soldiers stumbled and fell onto the ground, the others burst out laughing.

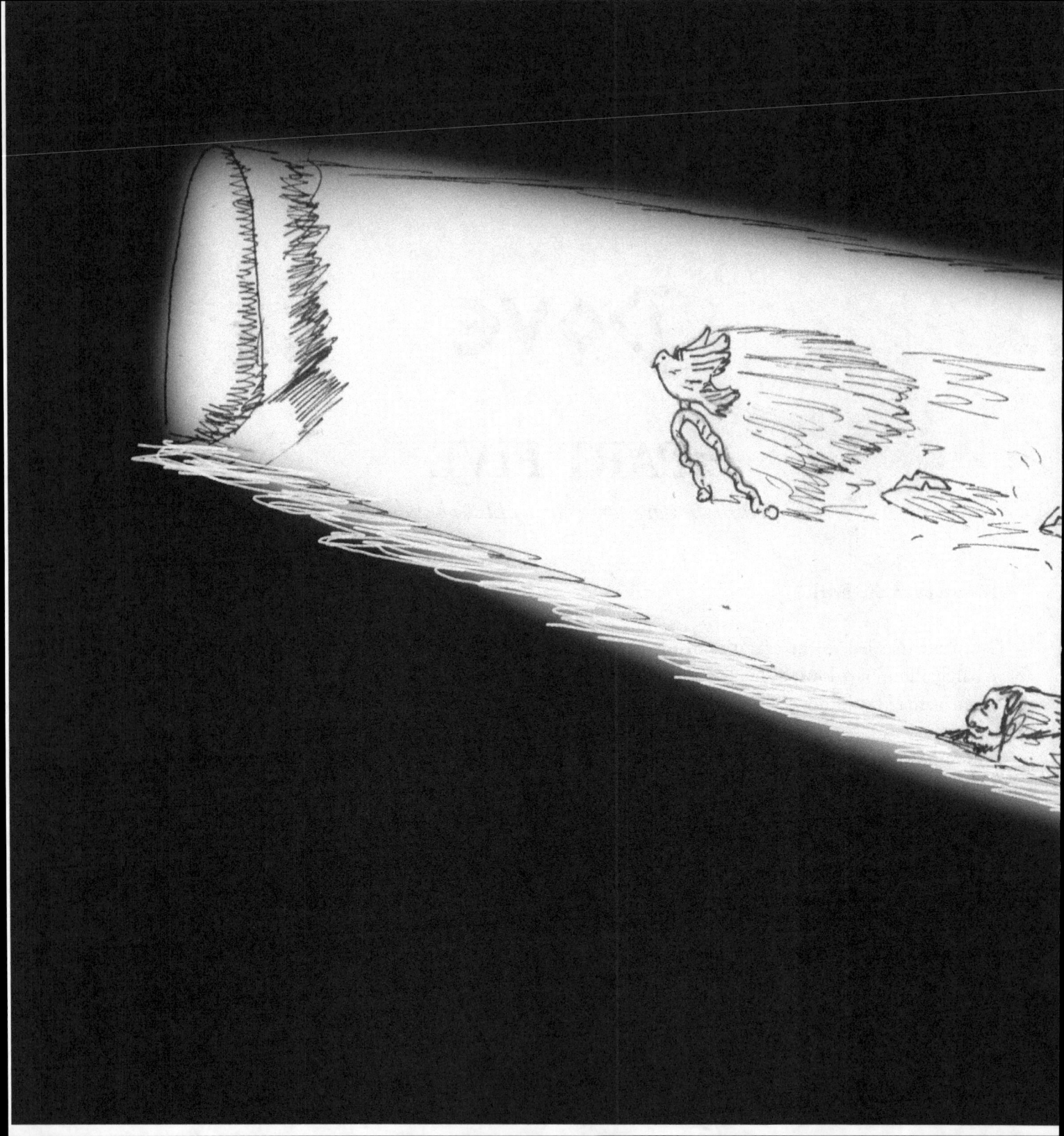

"Sh-sh-sh ..." Vashag wasn't joking around. He heard some-one's footsteps. Out of habit, Vashag raised his hand signaling his men to stop. But who'll see his gesture in the dark?.

The soldier behind stumbled into Vashag and both fell to the ground. All the others, stumbling one after another, fell into a heap. The warriors scolded the one who fell first. Vashag would answer them, but he was so pressed down that he could barely breathe.

The steps were heard again.

"Who is it?" A soldier asked.

"If you don't mind kindly getting off me, then I can probably guess whose steps they are!" Vashag said, getting more annoyed by the second.

Finally he got up, shook himself and listened. Not a slither of sound!

The steps were not heard. The cave was dead silent, and then again the sound of footsteps rang out, the steps moved quickly, running deeper into the corridor.

"They're running away! After them!" Vashag shouted and set off to chase the sound.

The Steps suddenly were heard going downwards. Without hesitation, Vashag jumped in after them.

The soldiers froze, listening to the landing below.

"Let go of me!" Someone shouted from where Vashag landed. The voice was male, squeaky and cranky.

"Who are you? Have you been following us? Or were you preparing an ambush?" Vashag thundered.

"My-my-my name is Gori! I'm a stained-glass window maker! I wasn't following you!" Answered the creaking voice. "I thought that food was thrown down to us. We've already dug up two bar-rels."

"What barrels?! I don't understand what you're saying! I can understand you probably are confused from fear." Vashag breathed and calmed down an little, as if feeling sorry for the man..

"I'm not confused! Here everyone must earn their food. We must collect the stones for the Dark Lord and put them in barrels. The guards at the top raise the barrels and take the stones. Then they put the food in the barrels and drop it through the mine back to the cave. That's how we survive down here."

The explanation was followed by an absolute silence.

"Are there many of you here?" Vashag asked.

"A lot, but I do not know how many for sure. It's dark after all. Usually you'll knock into someone in the darkness, you'll apologize, well some do, you'll ask their name and then you will part ways, never meeting that person ever again. When they drop down barrels filled with food, the sound from the blow is deafening. Upon the barrels drop, the convicts quietly creep up, take some food from the barrel and go on collecting stones."

Stones

The cave consisted of countless rooms and corridors. It, like a monstrous beast, swallowed innocent people and kept them in the dark, damp and dead insides of it's stomach. People who were exiled to the cave by the Dark Lord were inevitably doomed.

The guards threw empty barrels, and the convicts collected various stones and stacked them in barrels. Many convicts were looking for pebbles, in shape and weight similar to diamonds or emeralds. The poor people crawled on the ground and dug in with their bare hands in the hope of finding a stone that looked like a precious jewel. Others were looking for stones of unusual shape.

They went through hundreds of stones until they found something unlike the others, they would immediately hurry to put it in the barrel. They all believed that if they find a stone that the Dark Lord admires, their imprisonment will end and they will be released to the surface.

While Vashag was talking to Gori, another convict approached them and asked:

"Hey, who's here?"

"Gori and a group of newcomers." Gori answered innocently.

"Welcome! Where are you from?" Asked the convict.

"From the sunny city." Vashag answered evasively.

"I am a master of glass, I make stained-glass windows...I-I apologize, I used to make them. And who might you be?"

"Oh, folks like us specialise in wood carvings." Vashag involuntarily grabbed his belt, but there of course was no sword to grab.

"Anyway, I found a couple of interesting pebbles. I'll go and drop them into the barrel. I have to earn my food."

"Are all convicts in the cave either artists or masters?" Vashag asked.

"Yes. The Dark Lord hates our work and drives us here. He doesn't understand we could be of use for him." Gori said angrily, wishing for any place that isn't here.

"This is a very strange place." Vashag said.

He thought tensley, tapping his foot on the ground, trying to understand the absurd situation in which they were in: *What secrets are hidden in these pointless searches for stones? Why exactly are craftspeople imprisoned and send here?*

He turned to Gori:

"Leave us for a bit. Me and my men must consult something."

Twelve Convicts

Vashag leaned against the cave wall and sighed heavily. He had never been in such a difficult situation. The warriors waited for the leader to begin the council.

"I confess, brothers, our position is dire. It's impossible to escape through the mine. Its walls go up steeply at around five people's height, perhaps even more!" Vashag scratched his right side, the very same one that hurt from when he was pushed into the mine.

"Then what shall we do, Vashag?" Asked Yalov.

"I do not know ... For the time being we will work and make sure not to starve to death. I'll try to work and think about how to get out of here at the same time. We'll divide and look for each stone. Don't ask me which stones to look for! I don't know that either. We'll gather at the barrel, put the stones that we found in it. We'll wait for everyone to return. And we will look for the stones again. Is everything clear?"

"With all due respect Vashag, everything is quite simple. What is there not to understand?"

"The situation is very simple indeed, yet at the same time very difficult. It's simple for those who agree to crawl to the end of their days in the dark and collect stones for the Dark Lord, but difficult for those who want to change that."

"That makes sense. It is difficult no that you say it. I apologize ... I'll go look for stones" Yalov withdrew, stumbling and tapping others on the shoulders.

The soldiers parted and all went silent once more. Some time passed: no one could say how long for sure. Vashag returned to the barrel first. He threw the stone into the barrel and the sound of the blow echoed through the cave. Next came Yalov. He felt himself touch the barrel and lowered his stone into it.

When the whole troop gathered at the barrel Vashag said his name and then ordered the rest:

"Now let everyone say their names!"

"Chevik!"

"Yalov!"

"Atesh!"

"Shimshek."

"Voor!"

"Bahadur!"

"Dursun!"

"Elbek!"

"Chagrin!'

"Namus!"

"Yenmez!"

All twelve warriors were present.

"We will do this every time and if someone does not return, the whole troop will go and look for them."

Bird

Many days passed. Vashag and his comrades went to the cave every day in search of stones. Finding the right one, they would carry it to the barrel. They waited until all twelve appeared, and again dispersed.

It was the tenth or eleventh day of their imprisonment In the Black Cave. All had gathered except for Yalov. The warriors sat around the barrel, waiting for his arrival

Suddenly, the silence was broken by the clapping sound in the air.

There was no living creature in the cave except for them! Neither snakes nor insects!

Everyone looked up: in the faint light, a pale ray penetrating through the entrance to the mine, they saw a dove. The bird descended and sat down on Vashaga's palm. It was the postal dove given to him by Babir.

The warriors rejoiced at the dove as if they had met an old friend. Although the tender bird still annoyed the soldiers because for these mighty warriors any feathered creature, that is not an eagle or a hawk, must certainly be a chicken.

Vashag wanted to write a short letter so that the pigeon would pass the news to his brother. But there was no paper, no pen and writing anything in the pitch darkness still would not work. He did not send an oral message either, he feared that someone in the dark would overhear him. Vashag stroked the bird and uttered only his brother's name quietly: "Babir."

He took off the knotted bridle tied to his neck and gave it to the bird. The dove took the bridle in its beak and, waving its wings, flew up the shaft towards the sunlight. The guards of the cave noticed the pigeon and even fired two arrows at it, but they could not hit the swift bird.

THE CAMPAIGN

PART SIX

In which Elish embarks on a long and dangerous journey.

Alarming News

The tranquil flow of the feast was shattered. Talks at the tables were stopped. All attendees turned their eyes to the three uninvited guests, their appearance interrupting the glorious feast. The Khan allowed the guests to come through. The ruler recognized one of them. It was Babir, the eldest son of the minister.

"Babir, why did you leave the fortress? I trusted you with the Iron Gate. Did you get an order to leave the post?" The Khan asked severely.

"The rest of the garrison remained in the fortress. It's only the three of us here. I am ready to be punished for having left the fortress without an order. But first, let me explain."

"Speak!"

"Three months ago, a troop of twelve horsemen left the Iron Gate to the north. At the head was my younger brother Vashag."

"I already know this because I myself sent them to the north with the offer of peace to the newly-made lord of the north."

Babir continued:

"I gave Vashag a magic breed of dove, which the white mages still train in the Khan's dovecotes. Three days ago.

I found a dove in it's cage at the fortress. The dove did not bring any message from Vashag, only this ..."

Babir showed the Khan the bridle entwined by Elish. The Khan had already seen it once on Vashaga's horse.

"Vashag's bridle. No one else in the land had a bridle as ridiculous as his…"

The Khan motioned the chatty guest to be silent. Everything was now clear. If Vashag had good news, then the magic dove would bring an oral message.

"So the negotiations did not work out." The Khan suggested, looking sturdy and serious.

He took the bridle - there was no mistaking it, it was Vashag's bridle. Elish also saw the bridle. The boy was happy that his craft was still useful to the rider and at the same time worried about him. Although they hardly talked, Elish thought so much about him while he wove the harness. It almost seemed to him as if they had already become friends.

The Khan's Decision

The Khan, the minister, Babir and three thousand men left the feast and proceeded to the center of the Shah's palace. Waiting until all the servants had left them, the Khan said:

"Vashag never would have left his horse. And if the horse was killed, he would have put the bridle on another one. So he lost his horse, but could not find a new one. It must be that Vashag is in trouble. But why didn't he write at least a short message? He could of told the pigeon what had happened to him!"

The Khan carefully examined the bridle. He sought and was afraid that he would find traces of blood or cuts from the sword. But he did not find anything that would help to clarify the fate of Vashag and his troop.

"What does my minister say?"

"I will only say that I should keep silent. The Khan's ambassador is my youngest son. My heart is with him, and my head is full of troubling thoughts. A minister must have a calm and clear mind before giving any advise, which I at the very moment have not. I would like to leave the palace, as to not interfere with the validity of the final decision."

"No minister, stay." The Khan took a deep breath and begun pondering on an answer.

"So, suppose that Vashag lost his horse and sent us his one of a kind bridle. But why? It would be easier to whisper a postal pigeon a short message, and the magic bird would pass it to us. But why exactly did Vashag send the bridle, and not his ring with the family coat of arms? Then we would of known for sure that he needs help."

"And what if he's not in trouble?" Said one of the three thousand. He had no right eye, but the left danced around cunningly.

The Khan doubted this:

"Then why did he send us the bridle?"

The one-eyed man continued:

"Maybe Vashag wanted the boy to weave the whole harness for it to be send to him in the north. Perhaps as a gift to the Dark Lord? Most likely Vashag does not remember the name of the boy, so he did not whisper anything to the dove!"

"No, I cannot agree with you. For there is something more than meets the eye." TheKhan disagreed.

"Great Khan, the ambassador sent a wickercraft with a dove. Why would you think that Vashag is in trouble? I believe that it would be better to send the harness that the boy wove to the Dark Lord as a gift. And the boy, too, should be sent north. Just in case there something else that needs to be made! Let him go and then he'll come back with Vashag." The one-eyed man did not want to admit that something had happened to Vashag's troop.

There was a silence.

"We can not send our troops north. We do not have any evidence that Vashag and his men need our help. All we have is a woven bridle and our worries. If we send them a large army now then we will likely start a great war. And now is a difficult time, we won't be able to last through it. What does the minister say?" The Khan turned to the minister.

"Anyone who harms the ambassador must be punished. Whatever it costs us. But you are correct great Khan, so far we have no evidence that the ambassador was attacked or that he is in trouble. So we have no reason to send an army."

"Well we can't wait for the next winter! Great Khan, let me go after my brother!" Babir could not restrain himself and intervened.

"If you go, then you go by yourself. I can not give you any men, as I had given your brother!" Said the Khan.

"I left my post without your order. Consider this my exile as redemption of disobedience!" Insisted Babir.

The Khan replied:

"In winter, no army can overcome the steppes covered with deep snow. You have until spring. As the last month of winter comes, we will begin preparing for the campaign. If you do not return with Vashag before the spring holiday Novruz, we will advance with the army to the north."

"What about the boy who wove the bridle?" The one-eyed man smiled cunningly. "We cannot rule out that the northern king was impressed by the wickered bridle. Everyone knows that the Dark Lord is no different when it comes to art. I'm still sure that Vashag wanted to impress the new king and having sent a bridle, has basically invited the boy to demonstrate his skill."

"Looking after boys was not what i signed up for!" Babir protested. "I'm a warrior, not a babysitter. He will only slow me down. I don't want to be guilty for anything that'll happen to him."

"You were already guilty when you left your post in the Iron Gate. And as the Khan says, one should not disobey!" Cut off the one-eyed man. "Moreover, if you travel with a boy, no one will suspect you as a spy."

The one-eyed thousand grinned superciliously.

The Khan nodded his head.

"Take a boy with you, you never know, the harness might be of use for Vashag…"

Polite Invitation

The feast in the palace lasted until dawn. At sunrise, the guests began to disperse. Of course, those of them who fell asleep right at the table stayed in the hall and slept until noon.

Most of the guests could not remember anything from the night before, the bridle and Vashag were completely erased from their memories. None of them understood what had happened, since the Khan and Babir, who had brought the bridle, retired from the hall. An hour later the Khan, as if nothing had happened, joined the feasting guests, his minister politely bowed and left the palace.

Elish was tired of the of hearing the conversations and the sounds of music. Leaning against his father's back, he fell asleep. The father did not wake his son and carried Elish into the tavern.

In the morning Elish woke up later than usual. The bathroom was at the end of the corridor. Elish lazily stood up and went to wash himself: *"Every day you have to spend so much useful time on boring things."*

The boy went out into the courtyard. His father spoke in different tones with a man in armour. First angry then a lot quieter. Noticing Elish, the man tilted his head to the side and scratched his hair. Tears filled the father's eyes.

But the peasant put himself together and said:

Elish, the festival is over. It's time for us to leave this city. Unfortunately, you will not be going home with me. You will go with this gentleman to the north. You're twelve, old enough to go by yourself." The father stopped and wiped away the tear. It was evident that he was trying to keep his emotions in check.

Elish could not believe what he was hearing! He never left his native village. Horror enveloped the boy. Elish could not, like his sister, roar and beg his parents until they yield. He did not know how to, like his brother, fight them against the ground and yell, until he got what he wanted. Instead Elish acted, as always: just lowered his head, sighed sadly and stared at his bare feet.

"Son, I do not want to let you go. But they leave me no choice. It seems that your weaving will take you far from us, from our village. The Khan told you to follow his ambassador to the north." His father said in a muffled voice.

The father and son no longer said a word. They had nothing to say. With dull expression, his father turned and walked towards the road. For he was going west - back home, and Ilish had to go north - after his bridle.

"Do not be afraid little one. Nothing will happen to you!" Cheerfully commanded the man in armour.

In Elish's opinion the brave soldier was very self-assured. Looking closely, the boy recognized him as a guest who appeared at the feast with mud on his armour and with the bridle in his hands.

"You mean that nothing will happen to me, except for the fact that I will not go home with my father but instead follow you to the very far north?" Asked Elish.

"Our journey will just take a little while, after all we just have one thing to do! Don't be afraid!" Babir encouraged the boy.

The Silent Boy and the Chatty Big Man

Elish folded his few belongings into his hiking bag. The boy took two dozen of his best twigs and plugged them into his belt in the manner similar to a sword. He looked a little ridiculous, especially compared to Babir. Babir was a huge warrior with a face covered in scars, shining eyes of absolute fearlessness and a huge sword on his belt.

"I'm ready!" said Elish.

"Well done!" Answered Babir. "Now wait until I'm ready. I have three big bags to pack. You're sort of like a fourth, extra load that will slow down my movement. Don't be offended though, I just don't really understand why I need to drag you along with me."

Elish naively suggested:

"Why of course Sir, I completely agree with you. If you leave me at my village on your way to the north, it will be much easier for you to continue your journey."

Babir raised his eyebrows and bowed his head:

"Boy, do you seriously think you can outwit me and believe that I'm really going to do this? Or is it meant to be a joke?"

Elish shook his head: he didn't try to outwit Babir, and he wasn't very good at joking around

"But the question is, are you coming or not?! As the Khan had ordered. There, far north, twelve brave men are in trouble. Among them is my brother and I will help him!

I don't need you to accomplish that. But the Khan listened to the advice of the stupid one-eyed freak who thinks he sees more with his one eye than I do with two. The one who persuaded the Khan that Vashag wanted you to stand before the Dark Wizard and weave him some trinkets, and so apparently Vashag sent your bridle with the magic dove…"

"Did the rider send my bridle?" Elish said surprised. The magic dove didn't interest him.

"The rider? Ah, you're talking about Vashag. Well, yes, he sent me the bridle." Babir replied.

Babir tied up two bags to a short-lived bay horse, and the third to a tall black horse. He nodded at the bay horse.

"Get in the saddle!"

Elish clambered extremely clumsily onto the horse. If he were older, everyone around would have laughed, but given his age, others only smiled indulgently. The world around him changed when Elish was in the saddle: the people grew smaller or he grew up a couple of feet. Elish felt a little more confident.

To Saddle or To Halt

Elish proved to be more enduring than Babir thought. He did not whine or complain. He did not cry, did not ask to go home. He was sitting in the saddle busy with his twigs.

"Hey little one, are you not tired? Perhaps you want to rest?"

"It would be nice. It seems that the bridle seems to be a bit off and I'm finding it difficult to weave whilst rocking so much…"

"A halt is a halt." Babir said this with a look that seemed as if only Elish needed it.

Elish got off the horse and silently proceeded to weave. Quiet all around was something Babir was not accustomed too. He could not bear the silence. But to show the boy that he needed to chatter with everyone, it would mean to expose one of his flaws.

On the other hand, Elish rejoiced that his talkative brother and sister did not bother him with their chit-chat.

"It's better to spend the night here, but we'll continue in the morning. We must build a fire. I'll go collect the branches for the fire in the forest. And you collect dry grass or dried thin twigs, anything to make the fire. Will you manage it?" Babir asked Elish who was a bit spaced out.

"Will you manage?!" Babir repeated. Elish showed him the twigs that he wove. The boy looked at Babir with perplexity - after all, who else around here knows how to pick the right twigs so well if not him?

Babir was confused at first but then it hit him.

"I guess I didn't realise who I was asking." He admitted his mistake.

"Does he know more about twigs than I do? What does he understand about them? He can't even distinguish a willow twig from the vine!" Elish became agitated. But soon he plunged into the search for twigs of the necessary thickness and sufficient dryness. Yet now he had to look for not living, green and flexible twigs for weaving, but dead and dry for a fire, and Elish did not like this at all.

They returned to the fire at the same time: Babir with a large armful of thick gnarled branches and Elish with a bouquet of thin dry twigs. Babir folded them into something resembling a small hut, Elish overlaid it with thin, dry twigs. Babir took out the flint and lit a fire.

"We did a good job ... For a duo!" Said Babir.

Elish did not answer. He was already fast asleep.

The next morning, Elish woke up first as he was generally used to. He could not miss such a wonderful opportunity to twist some twigs, as they waited for him patiently.

Babir woke up, jumped up and looked around, a habit from his time at the Iron Gate. Dangers, of course, there were not, because they were still within the Great Land of Fires.

"In the afternoon we will cross the Iron Gate. If my comrades-in-arms recognize me, they will not let me go alone to the north. Over here, far from the Shah's palace, the word of the ruler weakens, and the sense of patriotic duty, on the other hand, feels sharper than ever."

Elish really hoped that his comrades would recognize their commander and some of them would join him. *"First, it would be much safer. And perhaps they'll send me back to Gyrusly, to my little quiet village."* Thought Elish warm-heartedly.

To Elish's great disappointment, when they got to the Iron Gate, there was a newcomer to the post who had never met Babir.

"Who is it and where are you heading?" Asked the guard. All his thoughts were absorbed in the beautiful blade that he played with nimbly, without even bothering to look at the travelers.

"Yes, I'm here with my nephew, we are going to the wedding of my relatives." Babir barely restrained his anger. He wanted to properly burn out the guard for such an irresponsible attitude to his service. Babir remembered the face of this muddlehead to teach him a lesson on his return. Contrary to expectations, Elish showed an uncharacteristic restraint and did not blurt out anything about Babir that would have betrayed him.

"Move along!" The guard lazily said. Babir spurred his horse.

After passing around a hundred meters, he burst out cursing. "Under me is a fighting horse! I'm sitting in the saddle like a warrior! Out of the those bales, the shape of my armor should clearly be visible! How can he overlook this?!" Babir rumbled like an agitated volcano. Elish, it seems, paid no attention to it: as he was too busy trying to weave the last braid on his new creation.

Cemetery of Ships

PART SEVEN

In which Elish meets Gulia-Bani

By The Sea

During the first night past the Iron Gate the travelers passed the sea: cold, gray and bubbling, like a furiouses desaturated lake of magma. Babir diligently avoided crowded roads and led them through deserted and abandoned places. He feared the scourges of the Dark Lord and also didn't to want run into any of the bandits who were robbing traders on the roads here.

The bonfire eagerly absorbed the dry branches, which crackled and hissed. Elish and Babir lay down by the fire. The shore was completely empty, although Elish also imagined snakes and jackals in the thickets of the reeds. The clouds completely covered the moon and thus the sea was not visible in the darkness, the roar of crashing waves fused greater fear into Elish's heart. Their small patch of land, illuminated by their fire, seemed for Elish the only safe place on the face of the earth.

"By the way, how do you know my brother? Rather, how does he know you?" Babir inquired.

"Brother? Are you talking about the rider?" Elish did not immediately realize.

"The rider? His name is Vashag. Yes, about him damn it!"

"The rider saw my basket, then he saw the fish inside it. He liked it. Then I wove a bridle for him…" The boy whispered.

"Wait, what basket? And what does the fish have to do with it?" Babir stopped him.

Elish was annoyed, he sighted and began again.

"We came to the lake to fish. My father, younger brother and sister, and me of course, began fishing. But to be honest, only my father was fishing, those two only interfered with him. I don't like fishing, or hunting, or fires …"

"Yes, I get it! Then what?" Babir interrupted impatiently.

"While they were trying to catch the fish, I began to weave. There was a willow tree growing near the lake; they have very flexible twigs, perhaps the best in our valley …" Elish stopped, saw Babir's irritated face and returned to the topic. "Basically, I couldn't resist and weaved a basket. You know, the one with the hinged lid, a double bottom, a fine mesh …"

"Well!" unnecessary details drived Babir crazy.

"You see, my father had the same reaction. He, too, like you, was angry. I had a fight with my siblings. The basket hit the lake, and nobody got it from there, everyone forgot about it. And then the rider appeared, your brother. He was very hungry and wished to eat fish from the lake."

"That sounds like Vashag!" Babir laughed.

"That day the fish weren't really biting. My father could not afford to treat the guest with fish from the lake. But then the rider noticed a basket in the water. He took it out of the there, and it turned out there was fish inside. We ate a tasty meal, my father cooks very well, even the rider said it! After we ate, the rider asked me to weave a bridle, since his was worn out."

Both stared at the fire, but each thought about their own things: Elish thoughtfully moved to his tent, and Babir tried to understand what happened to Vashag.

"Maybe you'll make another basket and we'll try to catch the fish in the sea?" Babir broke the silence.

"Here, by the sea, you can't find good branches …" said Elish, his voice slightly muffled from inside the tent.

"Don't look for the good ones. Use the ones you can find! We still have a long way to go along the coast. If we catch a couple of fish with your basket, then we'll stretch our food reserves for longer. There must be at least some benefit from your knitting!"

"Again they talk about benefit! Why does my favourite hobby have to be useful? " Elish said to himself and then responded out loud:

"It's not knitting, weaving!"

Elish didn't want to explain to Babir that on the shore he would find only clumsy and crooked roots, and that they would be too brittle. A true wicker craftsman will never make anything horrible. So he decided to keep silent. Sometimes it is easier to do what is asked than to prove that it would be better not to do it at all.

Along the Shore

Their way to the north ran along the eastern shore of the Salt Sea. The top of Mount Kaf stood on the left hand side. In places the mountains spurs approached the sea at the distance of an arrow's flight, but the path that led to them was quite far away. Snow covered the mountain peaks and lined the valleys, descending to the seashore. However, there was no snow at the sea - Babir was glad, since snow would hamper their progress.

For the first twenty days of the journey outside the Iron Gate they did not meet a single living soul. Babir intentionally chose the most eerie roads that bypassed all the places where people could meet them.

When Babir noticed fishermen ahead of them who were untangling fishing nets at the shore, Babir prudently turned to the left and, taking a big detour, went around them. Having avoided the fishermen who rose Babir's suspicion, they lost a lot of time and energy. By the time they reached the sea once more it had already started to become dark.

Babir found an empty grotto among the rocks and decided that it would be safe to spend the night in it. The high waves ran down the rocks and then splashed and crashed against the cliff face. The strong sea wind picked up the salty water and sprinkled it all over the shore. Even by working together, the fire that was made did not warm up anyone at all. Their hands shivered as if in shock from the chilling cold. The warm south was far behind them.

The bag with supplies noticeably has become a lot emptier. Babir asked:

"Well? Is your basket ready?"

"I finished it ages ago," answered Elish.

"Well, let's see it in action!"

Babir tied a rope to the basket and threw it into the sea. He was sure that he would easily catch a huge fish. Babir threw the basket several times, and each time it returned empty. Babir threw some bait into the basket for the stupid fish - a piece of jerky. But the greedy fish managed to eat all the bait and not fall into the trap.

After the sixth attempt, Babir's confidence was low. In the end, he was tired, he threw the basket into the sea, but did not get it out of the water. Babir tied the end of the rope to the saddle lying on the ground and went to bed.

The wind gathered dark clouds and the moon disappeared again. Elish was scared. He looked at Babir - who slept calmly and snored, attracting terrible creatures wandering around them in the dark. Elish curled up and lay down by the fire. He lay motionless, with his eyes wide open, peering into the threatening darkness. A couple of hours have passed, until he finally fell fast asleep.

Cemetery of Ships

The cries of the seagulls woke Elish. After a night full of anxieties and fears, a clear morning was the best gift. He left the grotto, went to the sea and washed his face. The basket was still in the water.

Elish wiped his face with his sleeve and spit the salt water. The boy turned around and saw Babir. He blinked around dumbfoundedly. Elish turned back, looked at the now visible sea and gasped. They were in the middle of a ship cemetery!

Throughout the coast, like the skeletons of whales, there piled up many broken ships. Some were so old that they left only shells with sea life stuck to its bottom, while others appeared to have come here recently. Between the broken ships there stood gravestones and statues with angular words written across them; they stuck up lifelessly, rooted into the sands.

"Where are we?" asked Elish

"How did we get here?" Babir asked similarly.

Babir was seriously worried, his eye began to twitch. Babir's concern was transmitted to Elish. The warrior peered at the remains of the ships scattered along the shore and stone slabs of tombstones.

Babir stood, stunned, as if he himself had become a gravestone. The ghastly wind forced him to scrunch up his eyes so that his face was covered with wrinkles. His glance slid from stone to stone, from one broken ship to another. He was looking for someone, for anyone. Babir walked briskly toward the nearest ship, or rather, what was left of it. He entered the hold through a wide hole in the hull of the ship and began to climb up the mast..

Gusts of wind tore up the dried bushes and rolled them into the sea. The mast swayed heavily in the wind but Babir had to try to get to it's top. He climbed so high that Elish could barely distinguish his face.

Suddenly one of the tombstones begun to move with an grinding motion. The stone slab stopped moving and then collapsed onto the ground. The clouds of dust raised by the slab quickly disappeared, and Gulia-Bani, the master of all wastelands and cemeteries, appeared before Elish.

Gulia-Bani

Elish was shivering. Of course, there was a terrible creature in front of him. His muscular arms were crossed across his chest, his face fixed in an incomprehensible grimace. His right eye closed, and the left running upward under the eyelid. The monster held beads made of bones, and muttered something. It seemed that it did not notice the child's sobbing.

Elish opened his mouth to call Babir - while the one on the mast was looking for something in the distance. AN real monster appeared under his nose but shouting would alert the creature, so Elish stood with his mouth open, afraid to move.

The silence was disturbed only by the muttering of the terrible creature and the howling of the wind. Then the horse made a loud noise. The monster stopped muttering and went dead silent, the left eye swam out from under it's eyelid and stared at Elish.

"He noticed me!" though Elish and bawled wildly.

The beast laughed. It laughed and Elish yelled ...

"So you finally decided to show yourself." Exclaimed Babir, descending to the shore.

"I decided to show myself?!" the monster was indignant. "You are insolent, Babir! This is my land, here I am the master! Forgot?"

"All right, Gulia-Bani. Don't waste your breath, we just accidentally wandered here whilst walking in the dark last night…" Babir stopped.

"Accidentally? I was hoping you'd come back with your debt. Or have I lost my mind and forgot how you ran away last time?"

"What is it talking about?" Elish asked quietly.

"Don't worry about it!" Waved Babir.

Babir stepped forward:

"Yeah, I left for a while, but I was going to return. And here I am!"

"Ha! You're here because you've got your directions mixed up and got lost. Luck is now on my side, and you .." Gulya-Bani's eyes begun to tear up, he inhaled air into his lungs and sneezed twice.

The superstitious monster was upset:

"Two times, two times! Sneezing two times is a bad sign. I think lady luck has turned her back on me"

The monster was afraid to frighten lady luck. When someone sneezed once, Gulia-Bani believed he was very lucky. But when someone sneezed twice, he believed luck was leaving him. The monster was generous and gave Babir another chance to improve his own luck:

"So you are a thief and a liar! But I'm noble, and I'll give you one more chance! Here are four stones." Gulia-Bani pointed to four boulders. If you lay them out by tomorrow morning so that they're not angry at one another's presence, then I'll let you go!"

Gulia-Bani turned and jumped into the grave. Babir ran to the edge of the grave and shouted:

"What does it mean that the stones don't get angry at one another's presence. You're deceiving me again, aren't you!"

"They are brothers, put them so that they are at the same distance from each other ..Ha-ha-ha.."

Four Seashells

Babir jumped on the boulders. He rolled the stones with fury, trying to arrange them so that they were separated from each other at an equal distance.

Elish from the side watched the warrior push the boulders with difficulty, pushing them with all his might. The stones were very heavy, and Elish did not even offer his help.

By noon Babir was completely exhausted. He dropped to his knees and stared at the stones. His clothes were soaked with sweat, and his face was pale and emaciated.

"Maybe you will first try to arrange four seashells first? And whatever way it turns out, you can then try it on the boulders. My father always told me to start on straws first. If you like what you see, then try with twigs …"

Babir felt stupid, as if he were a boy and Elish was an adult. At other times he would have scoffed at the answer, but now he has no strength to wit. Babir picked up four seashells from the ground and collected them in the palm of his hand. He easily built from them figures - lines and squares, but the stones still resented each other, because one was on the edge, then the other in the center. Babir laid out three seashells in the shape of a triangle and took the fourth to put it in the center.

"Stop!" Cried Elish. "Do not move it! A Pyramid. Then they'll stop quarreling, they will be at the same distance from one another!"

Babir froze: three shells on the palm of his hand in the form of a regular triangle and the fourth above them - the top of the pyramid.

However, this joy did not last long. Soon it became obvious that they could not build a pyramid. Each boulder was the size of a hefty ram and weighed more than one man could lift.

"That trickster, Gulia-Bani! Three boulders at the base and one above them. Who, apart from himself, can raise such a stone? To lift such a burden, you need at least five or six people."

Babir threw the shells into the sea.

"I'm sorry, my friend! But here our journey has come to an end. Gulia-Bani will not let us out of his graveyard."

Babir looked longingly at the sea. The waters have calmed down, there were almost no waves.

"Elish, let's cook something to eat. I'll gather up some strength, maybe I'll raise the stone." Babir tried to cheer up Elish who's eye's begun swelling up with tears.

Babir undid the ribbon of the bag with supplies, but getting nothing, moved it aside and again went to the sea. He wanted to check if any fish were caught in Elish's basket.

In fact there had been enough supplies, but if even a small fish was caught, it would please Elish.

Babir grabbed the rope to which the basket was tied, and pulled it out of the water.

"Hooray! Elish look! There's a fish!" Shouted Babir.

Little Fish

Babir tried to cheer the boy up:

"Come here Elish! Your basket came in useful!"

However, Elish was still thinking about tomorrow: what will Gulia-Bani do to them? How can they be saved from it?

Babir took the caught fish from the basket, drew the dagger from its sheath and carried it over the fish. He had already slashed a sharp blade across a fish's trunk before, but his arm, with the dagger in hand, hung in the air.

"Look, Elish! It almost looks like the fish is trying to say something."

Elish decided that Babir was playing him again - adults often say nonsense just to dispel sad thoughts from children's minds. But Babir's serious expression forced him to come and look. The fish really did speak silently!

"Do you understand what she's saying?" Babir asked.

"No, I do not understand the language of animals Babir!" answered Elish, slightly annoyed.

"Well, if we can't understand it, then we better eat it. Never had talking fish before!" Babir exclaimed, and he carried the knife over the fish for the second time.

Big Fish

A feeble voice came from behind it, from outside the grotto, from the dark depths of the sea:

"Her taste is exactly the same as that of any other fish! Let go of my child!" The voice was quiet, but unusually domineering.

Elish did not turn to face the sea but Babir turned around and walked knee-deep into the water. In one hand he was holding the caught fish, and the other was clutching a glittering dagger.

From the water, near the shore appeared the almighty back of a huge beluga fish. The waves ran against its sides, broke up, foamed and disappear. Large gold scales, straight lines from the gills to the caudal fin, glittered brilliantly in the sun. The fish poked its head out of the water and said:

"That little fish that's in your hand will suffocate before you decide what to do with it. Put it in the water right now!"

Babir plugged the dagger into its sheath by the waist and felt with his free hand Elish's basket under the water. He lowered the fish into the basket, closed the lid and loaded it into the sea.

"It won't suffocate." Babir concluded. "Who are you? And how do you know our language?"

"I know the languages of all people whose cities are on the shores of the salt sea. You caught my child in your basket. Release him and in return, ask for whatever you want" the big fish answered.

"Help us to get out of this cemetery and I'll let your child go!"

"As you wish. I'll be back at dawn and take you away from here. Keep my child safe while I'm gone or I'll come back with a little more than a way out."

The whale threatened and then disappeared under the water.

"She swam away? Who exactly is she?" Asked Elish.

"I do not know. Tomorrow we'll ask. Let's rest." Babir replied.

The Boat

In the evening, Babir once again checked the fish in the basket and then fell fast asleep. He slept as if tomorrow they were not going to face Gulia-Bani's punishment. Elish envied his carelessness. Elish himself could not sleep, as soon as the boy closed his eyes, frightening images arose in front of him: broken ships, ragged graves and, most importantly, Gulia-Bani's face. Elish felt the monster's oblique eye continued to watch them from the darkness. Just before dawn, he finally fell asleep.

At the shore stood a boat, and around it the sea waters were swarmed with fish. Babir awoke Elish and ran to the boat. The head of the beluga fish appeared from the water.

"Get into the boat. I'll transport you ... Just release my child," demanded the whale.

Elish reached for the rope to untie the basket, but Babir stopped him.

"Don't rush, think about it. Who knows what this fish is thinking? It's still not clear who's is worse: her or Gulia-Bani." Babir retorted.

"But she agreed to help us." Elish wanted to free the captive fish.

"But who can stop her from leaving us in the middle of the sea or drowning us?"

Babir turned to the big fish:

"Your child will be safe in the basket. Take us to the northern lands, to the mystic ghost-port. There I'll let your child free."

The whale angrily struck the water with its tail. Impressed by her power, Elish acknowledged Babir's worries: "With such power she could easily turn the boat!"

Babir ordered to take Elish to take only the most necessary things. Putting the luggage in the boat, he tied the rope to the stern, with the basket being tied to the other end. Elish sat down in the boat and Babir went up to the horses and talked with them for a while. Saying goodbye to each one individually. Then Babir shouted loudly and the horses rushed at full speed between the graves and the ships.

As the horses' hoofs hit the graves on the slabs, they stirred and screeched. From the stones, covered with sand and grass, came a grinding sound. One of the graves opened and Gulia-Bani crawled from within.

"Why did you let the horses go? Have you accepted your fate that you'll stay here forever." Gulia-Bani was pleased with himself as he noticed the horses on his way out of the crypt. Nobody except him could lift the unliftable stones and solve his puzzle.

"I don't think so!" Babir jumped into the boat.

Gulia-Bani was furious. He screeched so loud that Elish's eardrums almost burst. Gulia-Bani grabbed one of the four boulders, trying to raise it.

"There are no oars! How are we supposed to move?!" Shouted Babir. Elish still kept his ears plugged and did not hear him. But the fish heard him. She rested on the tern and began pushing the boat with all her might.

Gulia-Bani picked up the boulder and threw it at the boat. The stone flew over the heads of the fugitives and fell into the sea. From it rose high waves, and the boat almost rolled over.

"Can we pick it up back there, otherwise we'll all go to the bottom of this sea!" Shouted Babir.

Other fish joined the big one, and the boat rushed along the waves.

Gulia-Bani looked sadly at the boulders: there were only three of them left and anyone could easily solve his puzzle.

By Sea, through the Forest and over the River.

PART EIGHT

In which Elish meets the Black Bush

The High Seas

The boat had sailed far from the shore, so far that all land disappeared from view. Elish, having no twigs to weave, sat by the side of the boat, admiring the myriad fish that gathered around.

The big fish swam next to them. The midday sun was reflected in the golden scales so brightly that sometimes Elish had to turn away from the blinding light.

The basket with a small fish was at the very surface of the water. The whale swam up to the basket and shoved her head slightly. Her child woke up and began to vividly swim in circles.

After they had retired far enough from the ship's cemetery, the large fish with the golden scales never touched the boat. The rest of the fish submissively pushed the boat, and the smallest darted between them. When the boat slowed down, the large fish hit the water with its tail and the fish began to push more strongly, so that the boat again rushed forward as fast as the wind.

Elish was looking for an opportunity to talk with the big fish. Waiting for her to swim very close to the board, Elish lowered his hand into the water and touched the big fish, up to its golden scales. But as soon as he touched the scales, his fingers became numb, as if he had touched a block of ice.

Elish shuddered and jerked his hand away sharply, he lifted it and with his fingers spread out in front of him, he gasped: his nails had turned gold. Then the tips of his fingers were coated in gold! He began feverishly rubbing his fingers. Babir jumped to Elish and grabbed his hand. He did not know how to help the boy.

"What did you do to his hand?!" Shouted Babir at the whale.

"Do not be afraid, only his nails have become gold. If the boy hesitated and held his hand a little longer, it would of been really bad." The fish cut off coldly.

"So that's why you're so worried about your child! It turns everything into gold too, right?" Elish guessed.

"Not yet, but when it grows..." confirmed the big fish.

Diving under the boat, the fish swam out from the other side and, sticking its head out from the water, turned to Babir:

"You could have asked for as much gold as you could carry! And yet you asked for a boat."

"Sometimes circumstances can be dire and in our case an old boat is better than a chest full of gold. But the next time we meet, you won't get rid of me with a wooden boat!"

"It's not too late to turn your wooden boat into gold!" Suggested the fish.

"And let us sink, I don't think so!" Babir imagined how that would've happened.

"It's a good thing I didn't release her child earlier!" He thought.

"Do not forget to wear gloves when we go ashore. Gold nails will be excellent loot for bandits. Though they definitely won't wait until new nails have grow out and the old ones fall off!" Babir jokes, but when he saw Elish's frightened face, he hastened to reassure him. "Hey, I'm just joking around…"

From that one thought of bandits Elish already felt uneasy. He quickly took out his gloves and put them on.

The Coast

After three days and nights spent in the open sea, a long-awaited shore appeared in the distance as a thin strip on the horizon. Elish first noticed the land. He stood on his feet and jumped with joy.

"I've kept my promise. Let my child go." The whale demanded.

Babir reached for the basket and opened the lid. The little fish burst out. At first she swam to the big fish, and then headed for the boat. Elish lowered both hands into the water and stroked the small fish. His golden nails glittering under the water.

"Forgive me for holding you in my basket," Elish apologized.

Babir jumped into the water, they were close to the shore and the water was shallow. Bracing himself in the stern, he pushed the boat to the shore. Elish was eager to step on the hard ground: "Three days without weaving - that's too much!" He never parted with his twigs for such a long time. Of course, he liked the sea voyage, although capturing a small fish made him very upset. He felt partly guilty, because they imprisoned an innocent fish in a basket woven by him.

Babir's mood was excellent, humming something to himself joyfully. The journey through the sea took a lot less than if they traveled on the land along the coast. The ghost-port was very close. They left the boat on the beach and walked there on foot.

Ghost-Port

The ghost-port was in fact a small village. A dozen wooden houses lined the coast. There were several piers along the edges of the village; however, there were no ships or boats in the berths. Back in the boat, Babir told Elish that in the ghost-port the ships only enter at night and only ghost ships.

"Let's not stay here till dark! We'll get horses and immediately hit the road!" Babir shared his thoughts as they approached the nearest house.

At the port, you could buy basically anything, if only you had enough gold.

"You got gold?" Directly asked the owner of the tavern, in which they went in to eat and find dealers. Babir nodded slightly and the toothless mouth of the host grew in to a happy smile.

"Elish, I think it's time for you to cut your nails." Babir whispered gravely and nudged him gently in the back. "Two nails for two bearable horses. You'll still have three nails left!"

Elish turned away and put his hands deeper into his pocket. Of course the old man did not understand what was being said and desperately protested:

"What nails?! My horses can only be bought with gold!"

Babir laughed nervously and took out his purse.

"That's better! Don't know what those nails were about .. " The old man's eyes lit up at the sound of coins.

Babir counted out ten gold coins minted in the 'City-by-the-Sea'. On their front side were depicted two lions and the head of a bull between them and from the other side - calligraphy, saying: "Gold is not everything." These words were uttered by the first mint master when the great Khan offered him this position. The Khan liked the masters response so much that he ordered to mint all gold coins with that calligraphy on it.

The owner hid the coins in his pocket and dragged himself to the horse yard to prepare the horses.

"Ready to move on?" Babir asked.

"Do I have a choice?!" the boy thought. *"And why do these people ask questions, to which the answers are obvious?"*

"We went far to the north and wandered off our path," Babir continued.

"You said we gained a couple extra days." Elish hoped that they would rest a little before they continued their journey. The boy hoped that he would make up for those three days spent at sea, when he was deprived of the opportunity to weave.

"True, but if we loop through the woods, we'll lose weeks. Or more …"

"What do we do?" The frustrated boy asked.

"We need a guide. For gold, the local inhabitants are ready to take us to the Dark Wizard's castle. Sit here and I'll walk around the port and find someone."

The Black Bush

In Babir's absence, Elish decided to do what he liked most but discovered that the convolvulus he had brought was utterly worthless. *"I need to urgently find some twigs!"* In the dirt smeared window a thicket was visible. Elish, of course, was afraid to leave the tavern alone, but his desire to weave was stronger. So he left the tavern, turned the corner and headed for the forest which began at the edge of the village. He searched but there were no good twigs that he desired. Elish moved from bush to bush and gradually plunged into the thicket. Here, at last, Elish found what he was looking for - beautiful, straight twigs.

Carefully, Elish drew an amazing black stem, which his sharp eyes saw in the woods. The stem did not look like the other plants, it was flat and smooth and without leaves but with small dark maroon berries. The stem, winding on the ground, went deep into the prickly bush. The bush was bigger than his father's house in his native village.

Elish wanted to get acquainted with the strange plant. How can he not! He squeezed through a dense network of twisted bindweeds. On all fours he followed an unusual stalk inside the thickets and entered a tiny meadow. In the middle of the clearing grew a black bush, from which the same black stem grew from. Elish sat close to the bush and leisurely studied the unknown plant.

The black bush moved! He was surrounded tightly on all side by other bushes, there was not even a hint of the slightest breeze. Elish held his breath just in case - but no, the bush really moved!

"I wonder if it can talk?" Elish admired the plant, it's tender veins, black leaves and poisonous berries. His peace was interrupted by Babir's shouting. The warrior agreed with a guide and not being able to find Elish anywhere in the tavern, immediately guessed where to look for him. Of course, the boy is where there are bindweeds and twigs!

Babir accidentally stepped on the black stalk. The bush felt a touch and came to life. It quickly drew the stem back into the thick of the bush, and threw a loop around Elish, tightly wrapping around him.

The leaves of the bush were formed in such a way that the Black Bush took shape of a woman's face. Elish sat motionless as he was bounded by the bush's stems.

"Elish!" Babir was an experienced tracker, and it was easy for him to determine where the boy was stuck.

"Let me go, I did not hurt you!" Elish begged.

"If the man with the sword comes here, he will cut the root of the Black Bush!" Answered the woman's face.

"If I wanted to hurt you, I would have called for help! Babir could turn your beautiful branches into a heap of stumps in just minutes. But I'm not evil. I will not tell him about you. Fair enough?!" said Elish.

The black bush did not trust people:

"People are always deceiving! While they are weak, they pray for mercy, but as soon as you gain strength, your kind forgets about mercy! Why do you think I'm hiding here in the shade of the trees, surrounded by other bushes and do not grow under the bright sunlight? Yes! Because of mankind!"

Elish thought. "How dare they raise their hand against such a beauty?!" He was furious:

"How dare they touch you?! You are the most beautiful shrub I have ever met. There isn't an single crack in your stems. Your branches are smooth and shiny. Such beauty can be admired endlessly. I've been looking for such an ideal bush all my life. From your twigs you can weave anything your heart desires: harness, dolls, and any patterns ..." Elish spoke very sincerely, his eyes began to tear up.

The bush loosened its grip. The stalk curled in rings around the bush. However, Elish continued to praise the bush.

The sincere words of Elish strongly perplexed the bush. For the first time it met a human who did not see in him a malignant weed, a poisonous muck or a dangerous predator.

The bush folded the stem in the form of a hand and lifted it to Elish's face:

"Take my berries. Bury them in the ground and they will sprout anywhere. They do not need sunlight or water. You can weave with it's twigs as long as you want."

Elish gently tore three berries and, carefully wrapping them in a scarf, hid them in his pocket.

The Guide

Elish took the poisonous berries and crawled out of the thickets. Babir was already about to cut a passage through the thick bush and get Elish out. Next to Babir stood a short man with a slovenly beard and ruffled hair.

"Is boy the that... that's you talking about?" The guide asked.

The dwarf understood the language of Eli, but spoke poorly. He heavily distorted his words and wrongly built sentences. Elish recognized the individual words pronounced by the guide but the meaning of the whole sentences was often unclear.

The guide agreed for five gold coins to show them the way to Itil, the Black City. He demanded five more gold for taking them across secret paths through the thick forest.

The guide, following the agreement, led them along the roads, which no one went of their own accord. Babir, as always, did everything possible so that the slaves and spies of the Dark Lord would not seize them. He needed to get into the city unnoticed and find out where Vashag was.

Babir regarded the conductor with extreme distrust. Every time the guide chose a turn at a crossroad or offered to get off the main road to an abandoned path, Babir asked him to repeat again and again, he would make sure to match the guide's words with his marks on the map, and sometimes asked if there was another way around something. And so they moved: the guide offered and Babir accepted, and Elish ... Oh yes, Elish!

Elish, taking advantage of the opportunity, spent all his time doing his favorite hobby. Last weeks he had to weave "useful" things, and here he is again, left to himself and yet now he can weave anything his heart desires. Elish wove many things ... no, not things ... nothing useful ... he wove patterns. The boy began with simple patterns, like braids and stars, and then moved on to more complex ones. Sprigs and twigs came to life in his hands. The boy almost forgot to get off the horse, he just kept on weaving and weaving.

A week has passed since they left the ghost-port. All this time the guide furtively peeped at how the boy weaves. And so, seizing the moment, he crept up to Elish and, tearing the braided pattern from his hand, moaned with indignation:

"You are a artist... Good artist... Not good ... Not good ..."

The guide ran his spider fingers into the bag, where Elish had placed out the finished patterns, and took out a whole handful of wicker patterns. The dwarf stared at them as if he held in his hands not beautiful patterns, but disgusting creeping reptiles. With a revolting expression on his face, he threw them to the ground.

Elish became angry. He pushed the guide with such force that he fell in the dirt. The boy began to quickly collect his patterns. The guide got angry and rushed at him with his fists, but Babir grabbed him by the collar and threw him aside.

"Artist! Dark Lord do not like to draw! You can not! You can not! The artists all go to the cave ..." hissed the guide.

Neither Elish nor Babir payed attention to what he said. And that was their mistake, which nevertheless turned out to be luck. The guide cast an angry glance at his abusers. A cunning plan was born in his head: he will settle his score with them, and even earn a few silver coins.

The Abyss, the Tower and Two Bridges

After his quarrel with Elish, the guide behaved extremely suspiciously. Before he would easily concede to Babir, when he considered it necessary to change the path. But after the disagreement the guide became stubborn, argued with Babir, said that he knows better where to go. The guide would sway them, then whine and insist that Babir's obstinacy would lead them to death, once he even broke into a scream, but then he stopped short.

They walked along a deserted path among the tall, millennial trees and thick thorn bushes, when something happened that Babir could not foresee. The forest seemed to part ways, and the travelers found themselves at the edge of a high cliff. The trees grew so close to the cliff that their roots protruded from the ground and hung with giant fringes across the edge of the abyss. At the bottom flowed a stormy river, it's swift waters easily turned large stones, and the sound of their blows rumbled across the gorge.

The guide leaned against the ground and crawled away from the edge. With his hand he signaled to his companions that they too should lie down. Elish sat down and disappeared into the tall grass. Babir, who deemed himself too worthy to bow to the ground, took a few steps back and disappeared behind the fury of the tree's branches.

Through the abyss were hung two hanging bridges, and between them towered a wooden tower. The base of the tower stood on a small piece of land in the middle of the river. The tower resembled a sword thrust into the ground: a dilapidated hovel and a narrow platform stood on a thin leg of long logs that supported them. However the most important thing, patrols around the site. Because of the fog, Babir did not immediately notice the tower, but a gust of wind ripped off the white blanket and he saw it and watchmen walking atop. These were the warriors of the Dark Lord. Babir was very worried by the powerful sentry bows and their sharp long arrows: "Any attempt to cross the bridge without their permission is suicide! Archers will turn any brave man who attempts to run across the bridges into a porcupine with arrows instead of quills, in just a matter of seconds!"

Suddenly a man appeared on the bridge. "That's our guide!" exclaimed Elish. While Babir studied the tower and looked for a loophole, the guide jumped out onto the bridge. The bridge under the guide's feet began to sway and creak. Watchmen in the tower immediately took their bows and, placing the arrows on the bowstring, they prepared to shoot.

"Who are you?" Where are you heading?" Asked the sentinel.

The guide raised his hands up, but, releasing the railing, lost balance and the bridge swayed even more. *"It is better to be shot by arrows than to fall from the bridge into the abyss!"* Thought the guide dropping his hands and grabbing the railings of the bridge. The sentry, without hesitation, let their arrows fly. The arrows flew so close that the guide felt the arrow-head barely skim his ear.

"I am the Dark Lord's of the escort! I lead prisoners!" Cried the guide

"What kind of captives?" The sentinel asked.

"I do not know!" They are artists!" Answered the guide.

"Bring them to the bridge!" Ordered the watchman.

Shaking with fear, the guide returned to his companions. He understood that it would be extremely difficult to persuade Babir to pretend to be a prisoner.

Voluntary Captives

The guide fell to his knees, begging Babir not to be obstinate and trust him:

"Sir! To pass bridge patrolling permission without is impossible! If the believes sentinel that you are my captives, then pass are able we."

"You-you completely lost your reason out of fear!" Babir growled.

His eyes burned with anger, his hand clasped the hilt of his sword - one swing was enough for this heavy blade to cut the liar in half.

Elish thought that the frightened guide was about to faint. Elish put his hand on his shoulder to calm him down a little.

"Sir! I manage can to bridge you only as prisoner." The guide blew out.

"How dare you take us here you serpent! Find us another way!"

"Sir! You want the way the shortest! Here is it!"

"You did not say anything about the abyss, or about the bridges, or about these damn arrows!" Babir pointed in aggravation.

"Sir! If you say, is it then I change the way? But did agree you not to go get there in week one? To walk around the gorge you need or more two weeks! There no is other bridge!"

The guide overheard Babir's and Elish's conversations and knew that they were looking for Vashag and that every day of delay threatens to turn into his death.

Babir stood face to face with the guide and stared into his eyes. The guide turned away and continued in a trembling voice:

"Sir! You can exit bridge and announce the sentinel you who are and why you the walk capital of the Dark Lord. Then watchman might do not touch you. But then, the sentinel send the black raven with the denunciation, and then one day you will get grabbed and shackled and brought to bow to the Dark Lord!"

The guide lowered his head and fell silent. The naive Elish believed that the guide was guilty for having failed them. In fact, the guide was afraid that Babir would understand from his cunning eyes that he had conceived a cowardly betrayal.

Babir muttered something unintelligible and hastily retreated into the depths of the forest. Hiding behind a dense greenery, he approached the rotten stump with a large surface and spread out his notes and diary on it. He again checked the map, which he himself drew, and added a bridge across the abyss on it. After making sure that the way through the bridge is the shortest way, he hid all the papers in an tree hollow. Babir covered the notes in rot inside the hollow so that no one could find his records. He feared that if they were caught on the bridge, his papers would fall into the hands of the enemy. Babir accurately entered into his diary all that happened on their way from the Iron Gate, he described the large fish, Elish's golden nails, and many more things that would be very interesting to the Dark Wizard's thiefs.

When Babir emerged from the forest, his face was calm, his eyes cold. Having weighed all the pros and cons, he made the decision - he chose the shortest path. Naturally, the shortest path is always the most risky. Babir had no idea how much time his brother Vashag had left - even a small delay in the journey could cost him his life!

"I'll hide our weapons and carry them. And you let the horses go! Otherwise, they will starve to death." Babir ordered.

The guide led the horses into the forest, but did not let them go. He tied them to a tree and said: "Don't get bored dearies, I'll come for you soon!".

Returning, the guide shyly said:

"There is one more condition, sir. I have to tie you and your friend…"

After uttering these words, the guide hid past the tree behind him. And rightly so! The warrior's sword pierced the tree trunk just in the place where the guide stood a moment ago. Babir was not holding back!

"Sir! Not do kill me please! Listen! How, in your opinion, if I say to the sentinel that I alone lead two captives. And one prisoner is a great warrior, twice, no, five times more than am I! And why the prisoner's hands are not connected?! The sentinels will first laugh, and then turn us to shreds. Or, most likely, turn us to shreds and then laugh …"

From the rage that seized him, Babir roared like a wounded beast. Babir felt a dirty trick, but he had no other choice. He himself understood that no one would believe that this short man could lead two captives without tying them. The face and hands of Babir were covered with scary scars - mute witnesses of the fierce battles he fought. Such a prisoner does not calmer to threats from a man as small as that, and you can only keep him tied up!

"Fine! But remember, if you try to hold us, I'll kick you off the bridge with one kick!" Threatened Babir.

The guide linked Babir and Elish with their hands behind their back. With a long rope he tied Elish's waist, one end of which girded Babir, and the other end wound on his arm.

"Sir! You walk first, then boy follows, then I walk. So it is safe for-" the guide almost said 'for me', but stopped himself just in time. "-for boy".

The travelers came to the bridge and, reaching the middle, stopped. Seven archers, pulling their bowstrings, pointed their arrows at them. The guide turned to the sentinel:

"There are two convicts for Dark Lord's cave. They are artists! Here is the proof!" The guide took Elish's intertwined patterns from his bag and raised them over his head. Disapproving cries were heard from the tower.

"If run, shoot the boy! He the is chief, he is artist!" The guide suddenly shouted, pointing to Elish.

Babir turned around and was ready to fulfill his promise of kicking the guide from the bridge into the abyss, but ... Elish, frightened to the bone, was standing between them.

The sentinels fired an arrow: it whistled past the elbow from the boy's head. Babir resigned himself from attacking the guide or attempting to escape from the bridge or the boy would die. *Why did I agree to take you on this journey!* He thought, but he did not say anything out loud.

THE CAVE

PART NINE

In which Elish falls into a dark dungeon and finds a magical pattern

The Reward for bringing the Prisoners

So, our travelers became the guide's captives. The mean guide hoped that under the disguise of captives he would lead Babir and Elish along the bridge, and then, without releasing them from the ropes, take them to the Black Caves. Having thrown them into the cave, he will return and take away their horses and armor, unhindered. *"If I'm lucky, I'll still get one silver for the head of each of artist from the guard of the Black Caves!"* The guide rasped his lip.

However contrary to the plans of the guide, two sentinels from the tower volunteered to escort them to the cave. "One of the captives looks very fierce, to trust this case with a low-profile guide such as yourself wouldn't be safe." One of them said, hinting at Babir. Of course, they also thought of silver, which they would get for escorting the captives.

They were led to the north-east, straying further and further from the capital of the Dark Lord. Babir choked with impotent anger: *"Captured without a fight! I feel ashamed!"*. But what bothered him most of all was the fact that each step took them further away from Vashag.

Elish was burdened by the fact his hands were tied behind his back. Tormented, knowing that he could not lift a leaf from the ground or tear a twig from a tree. However, later he found something to do. His fingers groped for the knot of the rope to which he was tied.

The knot did not look like the knots that bound the luggage on their horses, and differed from the knots that he could see on the masts of ships in the 'City-by-the-Sea.' Elish studied the rope and the unusual knot, as if unraveling an interesting riddle. Of course, the boy unraveled the knot, but it never occurred to him to untie himself! On the third day they reached the Black Caves. At the entrance they were met by several guards.

"Be silent! I'll report it myself!" The sentinel barked at the guide.

"No! This my is prisoners!" The guide protested.

Another sentinel slapped the obstinate guide across the face, thus ending the dispute.

"I am the first assistant to the chief watchman on the tower at the double bridge. We have brought two prisoners," the first sentinel said.

"And what are their faults?" The chief of the security asked without much interest.

The sentinel showed the guards patterns woven by Elish. The guards twisted their faces and shook their heads, as if they had been shown some sickly muck. Elish was very upset. The boy is used to the fact that not everyone likes his wicker pieces, but this is the first time he's seen this kind of reaction.

The security chief threw a squeamish look at the patterns. The more beautiful and elegant the pattern, the more serious the accusation and thus the more weighty was the proof of guilt! Elish, of course, did not know about this rule that the Dark Lord made. Otherwise, the boy would not be upset of the guard's expressions. In fact, he would probably be delighted!

"I denounce him guilty!" Concluded the chief. He glanced at Babir and added. "And is this an artist too?! He looks more like a warrior!"

"Him too!" Interrupted the guide, afraid that the money will be given only for one prisoner.

"It's strange! A couple of months ago, we were send a couple of good men from the Black City, similar to him. They said they were masons. And in my opinion, they deserve a place in the Dark Lord's army, and not in the hard labor of the cave!" Replied the chief.

Babir lifted his head. He had a faint glimmer of hope that Vashag could be here too, in the cave. He shook his head and grinned to himself: *"No, it would be too much luck!"* He thought.

"All right, get a move on!" Ordered the chief.

Babir and Elish were led through the short tunnel that led to a sickly drop. They didn't even have a second to fear what came next as they were pushed into the darkness

What happened next would amuse Babir and even Elish if they had stayed atop a while longer.

"Sir! Will be I getting reward? The guide held out his hand.

"Scram you filth!" One of the sentries shouted.

Sensing the heat between the sentinel and the guide, the chief decided to keep the silver until they were sorted out.

"My reward!?" shouted the guide and, snatching a knife from behind his back, attacked the sentries. He knocked one to the ground, but the other knocked him down. They continued to hit one another in the dirt. A minute later the furious cries and clanking of the blades died down and three lifeless bodies appeared before the commander. "Well then!" He said with satisfaction and took two extra silver coins from the sentries pocket.

History of the Khan

When Elish flew down the shaft, his shriek was a greeting to all of the inhabitants in the dark cave. Elish though he heard Babir scream as well. However later on he stubbornly denied this. Once they had landed Babir absorbed the impact well and tried to reassure the boy, who was crying even harder. Babir had no choice but to wait until Elish calmed down. Finally Babir approached the boy:

"Hey little one, can you try untie these ropes? I know we're in the darkness, and even with bound hands, it's very unlikely you'll manage it. But can you at least give it a try."

Elish did not answer immediately:

"Yes, my knot wasn't that complicated. Yours is probably the same."

Elish easily untied the knots on the ropes, with which his hands were tied. In the darkness he found Babir and helped him get rid of his bonds.

"Where are we?" Asked Elish.

"I don't know. It seems that it will not be easy to escape from here. But we are sure to come up with something. I give you my word!"

"This situation can't get any worse," Elish said sadly. He remembered his native village, his barn, and all his unfinished patterns.

Babir felt his distress and thought of a great way to comfort the boy.

"Have you ever heard of the story of the Khan who lost his people? No? Well, let me tell you. Enemies ravaged his kingdom. His people dispersed through strange cities all around the land. But the Khan's spirit was not broken. He began collecting his people, like picking berries in a dangerous forest. He wandered through foreign streets in search for his native people. The Khan could not even utter a word in his native tongue - or he would be betrayed, immediately seized and beheaded.

Then he began to walk the streets of other cities and sing the melody of his native land, but the words of the song were in the foreign languages. None of the foreigners paid any attention to the Khan, who wandered about the city in a beggar's dress: nothing unusual, the words in the song were familiar! But his people immediately recognized the melody, although the song was in a foreign language. So he gathered up his people and brought them out of town, and then …"

"Can you sing that song? I'm not very good at singing…" Elish interrupted.

"I wouldn't trust you to sing it anyway." Babir said jokingly and smiled, but in the dark Elish couldn't see it.

They crawled along the cave, randomly choosing their path. Babir softly hummed the melody. Elish had never heard it, but Babir was sure that if 'he' heard this, then 'he' would respond.

Yalov

Elish and Babir did not know how long they had spent in the cave. Under the earth it's quite difficult to get a grasp on time. Elish tirelessly asked where exactly they are going. "Forward!" Invariably answered Babir. Unfortunately, this was the most accurate answer that the experienced tracker could give. Babir hoped that they were lucky and they would meet a fellow countryman, they could ask him about everything that had happened.

At the next turn, which the underground labyrinth concealed in it's thousands of tunnels, someone called to them:

"I know your melody! Who are you?"

"I'm from a city where the summer sun shines all year round." Babir's heart began to beat faster.

"What's your name."

"Babir, son of the minister." Babir straightened himself and prepared for a fight. He had many friends, but even more enemies.

However, the man in the dark was not an enemy, but a friend:

"Sir, how did you get here? After all, we said goodbye to you at the Iron Gate!"

Did they find Vashag's troop?! Babir jumped with happiness.

"Your turn to name yourself! Many people pass through the Iron Gate." Babir said.

"My name is Yalov. But you hardly remember me. Our leader is Vashag, your brother."

Found!

Vashag, after collecting a few stones, went to the barrel into which they were stacking the rocks. He returned to the barrel last, the whole squad was already waiting for him.

"Vashag?" Asked Yalov, hearing the footsteps.

"Yes, Yalov."

"Please do not think I am dilucinal but I must report that two guests have come for you ..."

Vashag was dumbfounded by what he had heard.

"Yalov, did you say "guests"? Poor boy, he's going crazy. Prisoners, who are kept in dark pits for a long time, start seeing visions, hearing voices, which in fact do not exist…" He worried about Yalov's state of mind

A third voice intervened in their conversation:

"Well, then, I guess I am but a vision!" Babir exclaimed and laughed.

There was a silence. Naturally, Vashag recognised his brother's voice. But how could Babir get from the Iron Gates to the Black Cave? "Maybe it's me who's going crazy and having visions?!" Vashag was overwhelmed by doubts. Babir waited patiently, his brother will come to his senses eventually. Of course, Vashag was glad to meet with his brother, but he realized that now they are both threatened with death. The pause turned out to be extremely awkward. Elish could not bear such moments.

"Mr. Rider! What's wrong with you?" Elish did not have the habit of interrupting into other people's conversations, especially the adults, but this silence was simply unbearable.

Vashag's stomach dropped. *This is the same boy who wove the excellent bridle for me!* He even remembered the basket with the fish. *"But how did he end up here?"* his thinking reached a dead end.

And suddenly Vashag came to a realization.

"The bridle! Babir, you misunderstood me! I didn't want you to bring the boy to the north! I just wanted to let you know that we were in trouble!" Vashag slapped himself on the knee.

He was very upset that Elish fell into this dangerous mess because of him.

Finally Vashag took control of himself:

"Babir, how did you even end up in the cave?"

"Isn't it necessary to look after your younger brother. I came to see how you got settled in." Babir joked.

Vashag did not appreciate the humor:

"Babir, why did you take the boy?!"

"The Khan decided that since you sent a bridle, you need a great master who tirelessly weaves intricate knots and loops ..."

Elish was pleased to hear the words "great master" in the explanation, although he was not completely sure whether there was irony in Babir's words and whether he was teasing him.

"Oh the horror!" Vashag grabbed his head. "I couldn't write a letter in the dark, and there was nothing to write with. Everything was taken from us in the Black City, and apart from the bridle, there was nothing on hand. But I did not expect you to send the boy to the north."

"Not 'you' ... but 'the Khan.' Actually, not even the Khan, but his one-eyed advisor. He strongly advised the khan to send Elish with me and the Khan agreed. I tried to dissuade them, explained that the boy would interfere on the way. But the word of the one-eyed wretch who lived at court, outweighed the word of a chief from a distant fortress!" Answered Babir.

"One-eyed advisor?! Did the Black Sorcerer mean it when he spoke of those who see with one eye better than I with two?" Vashag thought, but did not share his suspicions.

Berries

Vashag in detail told Babir about their misadventures in detail. "You've probably thought about how to get out of here." Babir asked after the end of the story. Vashag had stayed in the cave for a long enough time, but there wasn't a hint of an exit from the cave anywhere.

"The tunnel through which we got here, that's the only way out of here." Vashag pointed upwards to where the weak light filtered through the entrance of the shaft.

"We need a ladder." Babir concluded.

"Of course! If we had a ladder, we can climb up the steep cliff," Vashag agreed sarcastically. "Do you really think that it did not occur to me sooner?"

"Do not be offended, brother. But before you did not have Elish, the great master that can weave many interesting things to help us." Babir said proudly.

This time, Elish was sure that there was no irony in Babir's voice.

"But how do we make the ladder? Nothing grows in the cave. There are no trees, no grass, there are only stones. By the way, about the stones ... All the convicts are looking for stones, but no one knows why. It seems to me that we are looking for one particular stone. However we have no idea what kind of stone it is. Some are looking for a round stone, others - flat, someone is looking for a smooth, another for a rugged. The convicts believe that the Dark Wizard will let them go if they find the right one."

"And you believe he will?"

"No. He will not let anyone go." Vashag said without hesitation.

"Then stop wasting time and let's try to get out. Hey little one, are you nearby?" Babir turned to Elish.

While the two brothers were unsuccessfully searching for what to make the ladder from, Elish groped in his pocket for a handkerchief in which he wrapped the berries. He dreamed of planting a black bush in his native village. But this cave was the most disgusting place you could imagine. Elish was ready to endure the darkness. However, the complete absence of plants was worse for him than torture. Elish decided to grow a black bush in the cave and weave something useful. The boy dug a hole and planted the seeds.

"Elish, why are you poking around near the ground?"

"Mr. Rider, since I can weave different things, I think I can make a ladder."

"Of course little one ... I'm sure you can. But the trouble is that nothing grows here."

Elish revealed his secret:

"I must tell you, Mr. Rider, that I had berries, which the Black Bush gave me, who talks and even moves."

Vashag was very surprised when he heard about the meeting between Elish and the Black Bush. He never saw one himself, but he had heard rumours about the black bushes growing to the north of the Iron Gate.

"How did you manage to get it's seeds? The Black Bush is a killer worse than the Dark Wizard's thugs."

Now it was Elish's turn to be surprised. "The black bush is a killer? The most beautiful plant is a ruthless predator?

The bush himself offered me to take the berries with seeds. He said that if I needed, I could plant the seeds anywhere, and the bush would grow. So I planted them here."

Vashag started thinking. *"The black bush is cunning! He could take advantage of the boy's trust and, giving him it's seeds, migrate through the Iron Gate to the south, to prey on the innocents in Elish's village. And then, well ... It's terrible to imagine what the Black Bush is really capable of."*

"We'll wait until the bush grows up, then you'll get as many twigs as you need to weave the ladder, and we'll try to get out of the cave. I'll get two soldiers to guard the bush."

Three Voices

Time dragged on unbearably slowly. Day after day they brought stones to the barrel, waited, while all the rest gathered, and again dispersed. The black bush grew quickly, and Vashag's people chopped off it's branches and stacked them in a heap. And just like that passed days and weeks.

But one day Vashag, returning to the barrel with stones, discovered several people around the bush: two male voices and one female.

"Peace to you!" Vashag addressed all the strangers, who were hidden by the darkness. "My name is Vashag."

"Are you alone?" Asked a man's voice.

"My friends are with me."

"More hands - more stones. More stones - more food!" A second male voice said thoughtfully.

"I agree. Tell me, what kind of stones are you looking for? You don't just carry any stones around!" Vashag did not lose hope to solve the riddle with the stone and asked about it to everyone who he had stumbled upon in the underground darkness.

"I'm looking for a round and heavy stone. Absolutely smooth and without a single crack." The male voice said.

"Size of a palm, no more!" Added the female.

"You're not looking for the right stones! We don't need round ones, but rather an elongated stone, like an egg!" Argued the second male voice.

"And it is not necessarily smooth. There must be three scratches on it …" Interrupted the woman's voice.

Voices began to argue fiercely, and Vashag was forced to intervene:

"We are all looking for an unusual stone! But surely no one knows which one. So?"

"Yes …" all three agreed.

"I noticed that when we collect round stones in a barrel, they throw a little more food. Based on my observation, I assumed that the stone is round." Said Vashag.

"Or oval … We still have not determined the exact shape," the female voice corrected him.

"Ah, but precious stones like that do not exist. Both diamonds and emeralds are not round or flat. Maybe the stone is not at all precious?" Vashag tried to figure out the answer.

But he just couldn't think of anything

"But why would the Dark Lord not tell us what we're looking for? Then we can find it sooner!" continued Vashag.

"Unfortunately, only the Dark Lord knows the answer to this," the woman's voice grew sad.

"Who was the first to enter the cave? Perhaps he knows something." Vashag did not lag behind.

"How do you figure out who is first, who is second? Names aren't recorded!" The woman's voice laughed.

"Perhaps the blind old man at the bottom …" the man's voice went into a whisper.

"Who is the blind old man?" Vashag said curiously, he felt a step closer to unraveling something.

"We do not know his name. And he himself probably forgot his name as well. He spent so many centuries here …"

"Centuries?! Are you kidding?" The woman's voice laughed.

"What a joke! It is said that he ended up in the cave when the Dark Lord himself was imprisoned here."

"Was the Dark Lord imprisoned in this cave?" Vashag was dumbfounded.

"Yes. The Dark Lord spent an century here before he finally got out …"

"How do I get to the blind old man? I must meet with him!" Insisted Vashag.

"It's hard to explain where he's hiding. The cave is very deep. It has no end, no beginning. In the bowels of the cave there are a lot of passages and niches. We do not go down there. If you want to meet the blind old man, you'll have to go down to the bottom of the cave, to the underground river.

"The river?" This is the first time Vashag heard of a underground river.

"Yes, underground river. On its shore, that's where you'll find him."

"So you met him!" Vashag exclaimed, as if he has caught a thief red handed.

"No no. Once I stupidly stumbled down there. I wandered around for several days … probably … And then I heard man talking to himself. I wanted to say hello to him but I was frightened and didn't say anything. Then the blind old man stood up and went towards the river. But I was already gone before I heard what happened next.

Vashag and Yalov

Just a couple of steps from the barrel, Yalov's foot fell into a narrow crevice and he fell over, dropping the collected stones all over the ground. He crawled on the floor, trying to find the stones, but the darkness made all efforts in vain.

"If the Dark Wizard needs these stones so much, why doesn't he bring torches down here so we can actually see what we are looking for?!"

Vashag stood beside him and heard Yalov lamenting:

"You're right, Yalov, there's a lot of strange things in this cave. I thought a lot about why they do not allow us to work in the light."

Gori argued that the Dark Wizard does not want convicts to create, draw, craft … In the dark, they only collect stones to get some food in return!

"What if the Dark Wizard does not want us to see what we find? Maybe he wants us to find something important for him, but making sure we don't know what it is?" continued Vashag. "If the Dark Wizard had driven thousands of his slaves into this cave, they would have dug out and extracted all the precious stones in a hurry. But he only makes artists and craftsmen do all the work but does not say what to look for. So they are walking around, wondering what kind of stone to find. All convicts are convinced that we are looking for some unusual stone, but each of them is looking for a stone they believe to be the one, something unlike any other."

And then it hit them.

"Perhaps to find something unusual, you need unusual people. Slaves wouldn't have found such a strange stone, they would have passed it by …" Yalov dawned.

"That's why the Dark Wizard drives different craftsmen here. And they are all looking for something round, or smooth, or even some unusual stone. Everyone is looking for something that his hands remember. We are looking for a stone, which even in the dark, is immediately recognize by the hands of a master."

"But such stones don't just appear like that, they are created by the skillful hands of the artists and masters. They can't be just found lying around in the plains!" Yalov doubted.

"Unless someone lost it here..." Vashag was sure that the stone would save them.

"I heard from convicts that at the very bottom of the cave there is a man who had lived here for many centuries.

"Did you say centuries?! What kind of person is this? A ghost or an evil spirit. We'll go with you!"

"If it's a spirit or a ghost, then how are you, ordinary people, planning to help me? No, I'll go alone. I believe that the one who lives near the underground river knows why the Dark Wizard imprisoned us here. And when I find out why, then hopefully, I can learn of the Dark Lord's desires and attempt to use it to either escape or perhaps do something greater."

Yalov tried to convince Vashag to take him, but he was adamant:

"Yalov, while I'm at the bottom of the cave, bring two stones: one for yourself and one for me. And instead of me, you will call my name. I don't think anyone will guess that i'm gone. But remember, the Dark Lord has ears even in the cave. There could always be someone hiding in the dark and eavesdropping.

The Stubborn One

Angrily gurgling and puffing, Babir came up to the barrel, and with him was Elish, who, of course, was not allowed to leave alone. Babir laid the stone in the barrel and said:

"The barrel is almost full. Bring er up."

"Babir!" Vashag called out. "The convicts that I came across today told me something that will help us get saved.

Vashag told his brother the conversation with three voices. He told me that he had heard of a blind old man imprisoned in a cave long before anyone else, about an underground river and about an usual rock.

"So the stone that we're looking for for is magical?" Babir asked.

"I do not know. But the blind one who lives at the bottom, got into the caves long ago, when the Dark Wizard was imprisoned here. I'm sure he knows everything about the stone."

"Suppose that the Dark Wizard needs some kind of stone. Then why couldn't he take torches or lamps in barrels with the food? How many times do they expect us to hit our heads against the walls and stumble on the stones?!"

"I suppose it is so we do not see the stone when we find it. We put the stones in the barrel in the dark, like blind men. The guards raise them upwards, they give us food in return. And this will continue until they find exactly what they are looking for." Vashag shared his guess.

"And up there, where do they put the stones?" Doubted Babir.

"The convicts do not know. But when we were brought here, heavily loaded wagons, covered with black veils, moved toward us. I remember how once the wind tore the veil from the cart. So the driver, who led the cart, was hit as a punishment. And in the cart there was nothing of value, just a bunch of ordinary stones. Back then it seemed to me utter stupidity that he was punished for losing a bunch of rocks. But now the mosaic begins to take shape, and I see a part of the whole picture.

"But why doesn't he send ordinary slaves here, of whom he has plenty of? Why does he need artists and craftsmen?"

"Well, probably because the Dark Wizard hates their creations." Vashag said uncertainty.

"Why does his warriors and slaves hate them so much? When they were shown things woven by Elish, they nearly threw up. Do you think that the sorcerer's hatred is so strong that it was passed on to his servants?" Continued Babir.

"I have no answer to this question yet. When they saw Elish's bridle in the Black City, they also wrinkled their faces. Maybe the Dark Wizard thinks that only special people can pay attention to the special stone … I do not know …" Vashag began to doubt the correctness of his conclusions. "I agree, this part of the mosaic does not entirely add up."

"I'll tell you what, Vashag. In a couple of days we will have enough branches to weave a ladder. We'll climb the mine, we'll kill the guards and go home!"

"No. We must find the stone!" Answered Vashag.

"What for?"

"We must help these people. Here, in the cave, thousands of people, and many thousands in the cities … We can save them. We just need to find the stone!"

"These are not your people, not your cities!"

"It does not matter if it's my city or not. A beautiful song is equally as good in all languages. And if it needs to be saved, then we must do it! And also, if we leave the Dark Wizard unpunished today, we will inevitably return to a war torn land. If you had seen his capital, Babir. It turned into one huge forge, where do they take these swords and spears? Where will they send them? When will they finish gathering their strength and courage?"

"You're right! The Dark Lord will come to our lands with his mighty army. And that is why we will return and prepare for what is inevitable."

"Wars can be avoided if we defeat the Dark Wizard!"

"We are too few! Vashag, stop dreaming, come back down to earth. You had an order, but you did not fulfil it. I also have an order, and I will fulfill it. I'll take you home!"

"No, Babir. I'll get all the convicts out of this pit. You have to take my men and the boy home. I'm staying here."

"As stubborn as they get! It's a pity that it's dark in here - I can't see where your face is to give you a good old slap! I came for you, and with you I will return."

Dolls

Before going down to the underground river, Vashag had to figure out how not to get lost at the bottom of the cave. In this business, Elish could help out. Vashag was uncomfortable to ask a child, but he threw away his stupid pride:

"Elish, we'll need your help ... again. I'm going to the bottom of the cave. I want to ask you to weave the arrows to mark the way when we go down to the underground river. Without them, I will not find my way back."

"I've never made arrows, but I'll try, Mr. Rider!"

"Alright that's good. While me and Babir are down there, you'll stay with my warriors."

Elish frowned. He managed to become so attached to Babir and Vashag. Elish did not want to part with them.

"No, I'm going with you. Don't try to talk me out of it, Mr. Rider. Either I go with you, or I won't weave anything!" Fear gave Elish courage.

"So I'm not the only stubborn one in this cave. Okay, come with us!" Surrendered Vashag.

The black bush always tried to throw a deadly loop around someone's neck. The people who guarded him did not close their eyes and were always on alert. A couple of days passed before he collected enough twigs and vines and began to weave.

The young master had to try hard. What should the arrows be, so that the travelers can definitely find their way back? The tunnels in the cave turned to the side, then went up, then again dived down.

Elish almost despaired to figuring out how to tweak the arrows. He wrapped himself in his cloak and thought. Something fell from the pocket of the cloak. Elish felt the object by touch - it was the doll that he wove for his sister ... Oh, how long ago it was, since then it has been an eternity. And then Elish came up with a wonderful idea: *"Dolls can show with one hand where we came from, and with the other - where we're going!"* And he wove little dolls to point the way. Vashag liked it, and Babir, as always, laughed and said that he doesn't play with dolls. *"He's just joking around,"* Elish began to understand his strange sense of humor.

DEEP DOWN FOR THE STONE

PART TEN

In which Elish and his companions find the stone with a pattern

Descending to the Bottom

If a tortoise lived in the Black Caves, it would easily have overtaken the three brave men descending to the underground river. Going faster was just not possible - in the dark it was difficult to navigate. Elish stumbled at every step. In the end, he was tired of falling and climbing back up, he sank to the ground and continued on all fours. The travelers tied one rope around their waist to avoid losing each other in the dark. Vashag was up ahead, Elish crawled behind him and Babir closed the rear.

Elish has woven three dozen dolls. Vashag folded them into a bag and with these words: "Take it! After all wasn't it a dream of yours to play with dolls at least once!" Gave it to his brother. At each turn, Babir pulled out one doll and carefully laid it on the ground. He guided their left hand towards the way they were going, and their right hand pointed back.

The way down took about two days. Rather, they went to bed twice. Days had to be considered with sleep and waking - there were no other ways to measure time.

Babir continually lamented: "How can you be so calm?! This darkness drives me crazy!" Vashag's response was usually silent. Babir, as always, did not have the patience, he wanted to fight, to swing his sword around! But here he is, weaving through an infinite dungeon, and there's no end to it, no escape…

On one of the halts Babir put his hand to his ear and said:

"Vashag, is it just me or am I really hearing the murmur of water."

"I hear nothing. Your imagining things brother."

But Elish clearly heard the sound of water as well:

"No, Mr. Rider, Mr. Babir is right. There is definitely water running nearby."

All three, as if on command, held their breath and listened to the silence.

"Oh yeah, you're right!" Vashag broke the silence.

"Is this the underground river you spoke of?" Babir reassured him.

"Did you only now believe what i was talking about earlier?" Vashag said and spilled a chuckle.

Three Corridors

Vashag, Babir and Elish were in a huge hall, from which three corridors led. They in turn approached each corridor to determine which of them lead to the river. They listened for a sound and to the movement of the air. The murmur of water was clearly heard in the all the corridors, but which one to choose? Babir proposed to split up: Babir into one, Vashag to another, and Elish in the third. However, Vashag protested; he did not want to let the boy go alone.

"I share your concern for the boy, but we cannot all go down each corridor one by one. It will take too long." Babir said.

"You and I will check along the corridors. Elish will be waiting here. If these two corridors do not lead to the river, then we'll all go together in the last." Vashag offered.

Babir took Elish by the hand and said:

"You are a brave boy. But if you're afraid, then you can come with me."

"To be honest, I was scared from the moment I left my native village. I will be scared if I go with you, and I will be scared if I stay. But I'm very tired of crawling on the rocks. So I'd rather sit here," said Ilish.

"All right. Stay here. You can weave something to kill time…" Said Vashag. "If it's really scary, call us and we'll be right back."

Vashag and Babir went to each of their corridors. Elish stayed alone with his twigs and vines.

The Palace

Vashag, with his usual caution, descended the corridor. Gradually the uneven ground covered with deep cracks became even, like a marble floor. Vashag felt this change. He sat down, put his hands to the ground and was dumbfounded with surprise. At his hand was a step! The step was smooth, as if it had been polished by hand. Vashag held his hand: another step, then another! "A staircase!" Vashag guessed.

Vashags hand rested against a vertical line - on both sides of the staircase there were columns, even with vertical grooves. Inspired by his find, the warrior rushed down the stairs.

The stairs suddenly ended, and Vashag fell into the void. He flew down two or three floors and hit the floor hard. The hollow sound of the blow echoed through the cave. Vashag rubbed his bruised knee and, out of habit, turned his head to the right, then to the left, as if he could see something in the pitch darkness. However, naturally, he did not see the magnificent palace in the center of which he stood. The darkness concealed from him hundreds of amazing columns that held up the arches, majestic stone carvings under the dome of the hall, numerous staircases with beautiful handrails, curbs with embroidered patterns on them.

A husky voice, which came from the darkness, made Vashag shudder:

"Let me introduce myself. My name is Echo. And this is my palace. I built it for many years. I assure you, my palace is the most beautiful in the world. Do you like it?

"I can not appreciate its beauty without light." Vashag said.

"Oh yeah! No one but me can see it. The whole palace, it's every corner in my memory. I remember every stone, every step. The palace became a part of me. I see it without even looking. After all one does not need to look at their hand to feel it, to know if your fingers are protruding or are clenched into a fist. And thus you can say I see my palace without eyes.

About that! It was the Dark Lord who ripped out my eyes. Now I'm blind. But in here, in total darkness, it does not matter. The darkness tends to call the blind and the sighted. Won't you agree?"

He was very close. Vashag could even feel Echo's breath.

Then there was a roar. Someone fell from the ceiling.

"Ah! This darned cave!" It was Babir.

"Babir!" Vashag called to his brother.

Turns out both of the corridors led to the same hall.

"Welcome." Echo greeted Babir.

"Vashag! Who in the hell is that?" Babir did not like his conventions and riddles.

"I am the master of this palace and its only inhabitant." Echo declared proudly. "Be careful! You have a river behind you!"

Echo was a great fan of chatting and now anticipated a long conversation with his new friends.

"Vashag, did you ask him about the stone already?" Babir inquired.

Echo intervened:

"What kind of stone?"

Vashag did not give Babir the opportunity to be rude and answered himself:

"We came for a stone that the Dark Wizard is looking for. Can you please tell us where to find it."

Babir, stealthily, took a few steps towards Vashag. His brother's voice helped him move in the dark, like a beacon in the sea.

"Why should I tell you where the stone is?" Echo asked indifferently.

"Because it you don't we're going to pummel your ugly face!" Blurted Babir.

Echo laughed.

"In the dark? You are blind here. And i myself, guess you can say, can see! I know my palace, like you know your five fingers! How will you catch me?" Babir's threats were pushed aside by Echo.

Vashag hastened to direct the conversation in a more tranquil direction:

"My brother got excited! I'm curious what's special about this stone! Why does the Dark Wizard want to possess it so passionately? If, of course, this is not a secret …"

"Why yes off course, It is a big secret! But not for you. You, i guess you can say, are a dead men walking. For there is no way out of my palace. There are a lot of entrances, but they are all on the ceiling …" Echo laughed. "You can not get to the ceiling. The palace has high walls and a large dome! If you do not have wings then you can not fly to the ceiling, and you will stay here forever! But the good thing is that now you can't get out of here, meaning, that I will reveal to you all of my secrets. What kind of secrets would the dead like to hear…"

Echo walked shuffling in a gait around the hall.

"So, you asked about the stone. The stone is not magic at all. The only unusual thing about it is that it is completely round."

Vashag was disappointed: "How?! An ordinary stone?!"

Echo continued:

"But there's a pattern on the stone. Many centuries ago, the Great Magician traced a pattern on the stone as a spell against the Dark Lord. The Dark Lord is helpless before the pattern. If the Dark Lord or any of his slaves were to look at the pattern, they lose their strength, their hearts fill with fear. When the Great Magician's time came to an end, he decided to save his people from the Dark Lord. The Great Magician imprisoned the Dark Lord in this cave. Of course, then the cave was not yet turned into a magnificent palace. The Great Magician inserted a stone with the pattern in the masonry of the entrance, which was walled in so that the pattern was turned into the interior of the cave and Dark Lord could not even move from fear. He spent many centuries here, crying in the darkness and loneliness. He did not approach the entrance to the cave, because he was so afraid of the pattern protecting it.

"And who was the one who opened the entrance! Who was the one who let him escape? Who is this clever idiot?!" Interrupted Babir.

"Me! I was looking for gemstones. Seeing the walled entrance to the cave, I thought that there was a treasure hidden behind it. I hacked the entrance. The stone with the pattern fell and rolled down the cave. The Dark Lord jumped out and ran. But soon returned, frightened that I had time to see the pattern on the stone. The Dark Lord flashed his staff. He wanted to burn me and turn me into ashes. I dodged, but the bright flames distracted me from his next move, he grabbed my face and ripped out my eyes so if i found the pattern again, I would not see it. I fell unconscious from the pain and he threw me deep into the cave. The Dark Lord blocked the entrance with stones so that I would remain forever underground. I found the stone and carried it to the bottom of the cave. I hid there for centuries, alive by the stones faint magic. And then I realized that since I live in a cave, I need a house. And so I built a house, then I increased it. Finally, I decided that I needed a palace. And now I have the most beautiful palace ever created by human hands. And only my hands! No one can take it away from me. Even the Dark Lord can not take my palace, as long as the stone with the pattern is with me."

"You mean the stone is here?" Babir heard what he wanted.

"Yes." Echo regretted blurting out too much.

Vashag whispered into Babir's ear:

"It won't be difficult to find the stone. Here all the stones are either flat or faceted. This madman has carved steps and columns from them. A stone with a pattern is the only one that he would not dare to spoil!"

Echo heard Vashag's words. Over the years spent in the dark, his hearing was better than that of an owl.

"Look, look! When you find it, you can keep it for yourself. Though you're not allowed to carry it away!" Echo laughed again.

"If we can not get out of your palace, then reveal other secrets to us. Tell me, why does the Dark Wizard hate artists and craftsmen so much? Why does he bring them here?" Vashag asked.

There was a sound of shuffling. Echo walked back and forth, wondering whether to him tell or not.

"Whatever, all the same, you are dead anyway. Artists, craftsmen, all those who paint or decorate ... In general, they all draw patterns and ..." Echo stopped.

"So, what is next?"

"They can accidentally draw the same pattern, well, the one that is engraved in the stone ... After all, the pattern is simple … Then the Dark Lord will really have a hard time!"

"So, it's not the stone at all? It's the pattern!" exclaimed Vashag.

"That's why the Dark Wizard makes us look for the stone in the dark! So that we do not see the pattern when we find the stone!" The puzzle was almost complete, the darkness of the mystery dissipated.

"Echo, if you are afraid of the Dark Wizard, then the most sensible thing is to give the stone to us and help us get out. If we defeat the Dark Wizard with the help of then stone, then you will not be afraid of him anymore." Vashag persuaded Echo.

"Be silent! I already got too muddled up and told you too much! Do not forget that it was the Dark Lord who ripped out my eyes! He gave me the opportunity to see in the dark! Thanks to the Dark Lord I have this palace!"

Vashag had no hope to convince Echo:

"You stayed in the cave for a long time and forgot how beautiful the world is outside, how the grass smells and the birds sing! We'll get you out."

Echo lost his patience and went on shouting:

"I said be silent! I know what you want! You want the same as all the others who came down here! You want to deprive me of my palace! But you will not do anything! You will die here like the ones that came before you!"

Flying Stones

While Vashag spoke to Echo, Babir crawled around the hall on his fours. He was looking for the only round stone among the thousands of flawless straight cubes crafted by the insane Echo. For many years, Echo worked with the round stones brought to him by the underground river. Day after day, he turned them into even cubes for the construction of his palace. Babir could not believe that all this was done by one person!

Whilst Echo was boiling more and more, then praising his palace, then threatening the guests. The blind madman became so excited that he did not notice how Babir was fumbling around on the floor in search of the stone - round, with a magical pattern.

When Babir's hand came across the same stone with the pattern, he recognized it at once and understood that that was it. Among the thousands of stones turned by Echo's caring hands into regular rectangular cubes, this one stone remained in its original form, perfectly round and flawless.

Babir hastily felt the stone, hoping to unravel the pattern. To his chagrin, there were no cuts or scratches on the stone. Babir, trying not to make noise, put the stone in his bag and returned to Vashag.

"I think I found it …" Babir whispered to Vashag.

Echo's ears absorbed the echoing of Babir's words. He screamed angrily. Echo did not expect that his guests would find the stone in the utter darkness. In a fit of mad anger, he picked up a stone cube from the floor and threw it at Babir with all his might. The stone hit the column behind them and shattered into small pieces.

Babir and Vashag stood helpless, like blind kittens, they couldn't possibly predict where they will be hit. The next stone got Vashag in the leg. He cried out in pain and fell. Another stone hit Babir in the shoulder.

"He will clobber us to death …" Babir said through the pain.

Savior

As always, at the most crucial and difficult times, help came from the most unexpected ways. The two brothers lost all hope of escaping from Echo's palace. Suddenly Babir felt someone's touch. He turned with a catlike dexterity and tried to grab him. But in his hand was not the madman's fingers reaching for his throat, but … a rope. Yes, the most common rope, woven from the branches of the Black Bush with strong double knots, which Elish likes to tie. The rope hung down from the entrance of the ceiling.

Elish did not wait for Babir with Vashag and decided that he himself would go through the third corridor. Unlike Babir and Vashag, he crawled. Having reached the entrance, Elish stopped at the edge. The boy heard the whole conversation between Vashag and Echo. Elish hastily wove a rope and sent it down into the palace.

"Vashag, grab the rope! It's Elish!" Babir rejoiced.

He helped his brother and followed behind. Vashag and Babir quickly climbed the rope. Up above, Elish was waiting for them.

Echo was in utter confusion. He did not understand where his guests had disappeared: *"Did they really have wings and fly away?!"*

The Rope

Vashag's men, replacing each other, carried a patrol on the Black Bush. Blows from heavy stones prevented the wild growth of the plant. They tirelessly chopped all the growing stems and branches of the carnivorous bush.

The soldiers met Elish and his two caring guardians with cheers. The news of the stone found by Babir inspired them. They took turns handing it over from hand to hand, the stone that the Dark Wizard feared so much. Everyone was trying to understand what was so special with the stone. But the darkness hid the pattern left on the stone by the Great Magician.

"So, we have the stone. All that remains is to figure out how to get out." Babir said, taking the stone from Yalov's hands.

"I know how to get out! I only need a rope!" Yalov, as always, wanted to excel.

"We have a rope!" Babir did not see Elish, but he was sure that the boy smiled when he heard these words. "I think it will be better if you tell me how to get up the shaft. It goes straight up, but in the dark I don't think you'll see what to hook onto on the wall.

"I will not climb the mine! The guards themselves will raise me. Together with the barrel." Yalov said followed by a short pause. "When I'm up there, I'll hook one end of the rope over the cracks in the rock and I'll drop the other end to you."

"And what will happen to you?" Vashag asked.

"They'll take me for a fugitive, they'll hit me and push me back down here." Yalov said without a shadow of fear.

Yalov offered the only possible way to escape from the cave. But for the young daredevil the punishment might in fact not be flogging, but possibly a severed head.

"Well, let's try it." Vashag said with a heavy heart as he accepted Yalov's offer.

Elish wove a strong double rope with large knots that intercepts through each elbow. Yalov wound the end of the rope on a stone and pulled it into a tight knot. It turned out to be a stone anchor. Climbing up, Yalov had to place the anchor in the crevice between the rocks so that the anchor was stuck there. Yalov sat down in the barrel. Babir, Vashag and the rest of the soldiers settled around the barrel. Elish was weaving something from the Black Bushes branches..

It did not take long to wait: at the top there was a grinding drum, on which the rope wound. The barrel, tearing itself away from the ground, began to climb the shaft. Elish heard the winch grunting and the rope pulling. He involuntarily released the twigs from his hands and clamped his ears.

Waiting for the barrel to come up to the platform with which they were thrown down. The barrel stopped. A second passed and Yalov jumped out of the barrel. He had very little time! The guard, finding an empty barrel, rushed to look for the fugitive. Yalov smashed the stone anchor into the crevice in the rock, and the stone settled deeply there. Yalov yanked at the rope, but the anchor did not budge. "It's strong!" Yalov threw the rope down, and he ran towards the exit. It was important that he was mistaken for a fugitive and was not suspected of preparing an escape.

"The barrel is empty!" Shouted the guard.

"Can not be! The barrel was heavy! I could barely lift it!" The other objected.

"Fools! One of the convicts is trying to escape!" Again the chief guard tried preventing the escape.

The guards drew their swords and moved towards the mine. Yalov jumped out to meet them. He tried to sneak past them. The chief of security put his foot up, and Yalov, stumbling, fell to the ground. The guards pounced on him and, grabbing his hands, led him outside.

The light, though weak, in the evening, painfully blinded his eyes. For all the time spent in the dark cave, the eyes are completely out of touch with the sunlight. Yalov covered his face with his hands and lowered his head.

"Chief, is this not one of those tall masons, the ones that were brought in the late summer?" Squeaked a thin, long guard.

"Right!" The chief of the guards agreed. "I told you they do not belong here! They should be slaves, Yes! I wish they joined the Dark Army!"

"And what shall we do with him? Back to the cave?" Asked the guard.

The chief squatted down in front of Yalov and raised the handle of the whip over his head. The warrior removed his hands from his face and stared directly at the boss. In Yalov's glance there was so much fury and audacity that the chief jerked back and landed on his soft spot.

"We'll figure out in the morning! In the meantime, bind him and throw him into the stable!" Ordered the chief, walking away ashamed.

Blind and Sighted

Babir grabbed the rope with both hands and hung on it. Having made sure of the ropes strength, he planted Elish on his back and prepared to go up.

"Babir, you will go last! The boy is with you ..." Said Vashag, as if he saw his brother in the dark. "I'll go first, then the rest of you."

Strangely enough, Babir did not bicker.

"It's already dark outside. We are used to the darkness, but there are no guards. This is our chance!" Continued Vashag.

He scrambled up the rope and threw down a pebble - a sign to the rest to follow him. A minute later the troop had climbed up. Babir with Elish on his back climbed last

"Ready?" Vashag asked.

"Yes!" Replied the troop in chorus.

"Little one, you get off me. Wait here while the adults sort out some business!" Babir lowered Elish to the ground.

The soldiers, armed with cobblestones, headed for the exit. Elish did not hurry outside. The battle did not interest him, especially since he could not stand blood. For a while, the clatter of swords and the deafening sounds from the stones were heard from the outside, but soon they were replaced by dead silence. The battle was very short. The fugitives easily defeated the guards of the cave. Months spent in the dark, sharpened the vision of Vashag and his warriors. In the black of night, the guards had no more chances than blind puppies against a pack of wolves.

Elish cautiously stepped over the bodies spread out on the cold earth and walked into the lodge. Once inside the room, Elish quickly counted his companions: "Babir, Vashag, all the warriors ...We are all safe!".

Babir studied the armor and weapons of the guards. They were very different from those used in the south.

"What's next, Vashag?" Babir said with an long heavy sword in his hands.

"We must go to the Black City!" Replied Vashag without hesitation

"I knew that you were going to say that! You will not calm down until you achieve your goal."

Babir took his sword and pointed towards Vashag's face.

"But I won't agree to it!" Babir said in an impassioned tone. "I'm the older brother. And I have one last order from the Khan! We'll spend the night in the lodge, and in the morning we are all going home."

Freedom

The warriors locked themselves in the lodge and fell asleep, forgetting to set sentries. An unprecedented carelessness! Everyone was so tired that no one remembered the stone that Babir had gotten with great difficulty. Nobody except Elish. When everyone fell asleep, the boy secretly took out the stone and brought it to the window. In the moonlight he saw the magical distinguishable pattern.

Lovingly admiring the pattern, the boy hugged the stone and fell asleep. Elish, the very same boy that complained of restless sleep and would wake up ten times a night, slept like a bunny. He didn't stop even with the loud snoring of a dozen big men!

In the morning, when the sun was shining outside the windows and early birds were singing, suspicious sounds were heard from outside. Someone was wandering around the lodge. And not one! Sounds came from all sides.

Babir woke up first. He drew his sword from his scabbard, crouched and approached Vashag:

"Vashag, wake them up! We're surrounded!"

Elish heard the last word through his sleep: "... *surrounded!*". The boy just calmed down and was sure that the worst was over and ahead of them was a pleasant journey home. And now the restless thoughts filled his poor head again: "Who surrounded us? What are they going to do with us?"

The soldiers drew their swords and prepared for battle. Vashag knocked the door open and screamed out of the lodge. The others poured out after him, pushing. Elish followed on very closely behind Babir.

Only instead of cruel warriors of the Dark Lord they saw pale and emaciated women and men, young and old! They were poor convicts, prisoners of the Black Cave. They used the rope made by Elish and raised up by Yalov. But being at large, they did not know what to do next. After all, they were artists and craftsmen, their nature was subtle, they were good dreamers and conscientious workers. But not warriors! They were not familiar with the military business, they never held weapons in their hands. And most importantly, they did not have a leader. The convicts sat near the lodge all night until morning, waiting for their liberators.

"Sir, do you recognize me?" One of the convicts addressed to Vashag.

"Yes, Gori, I recognize your voice!" Vashag answered happily.

Vashag imagined him as a hunched old man, yet Gori turned out to be a young tall fellow with kind, alive eyes. It's an amazing feeling when you meet a person for the first time with to whom you have talked for a long time, but never saw. You start to paint a portrait in your mind, imagining his face. But when the time comes for the first meeting, surprises usually await.

One word was enough for Vashag to recognize the rest of his friends: a squeaky voice belonged to a decrepit potter, a young sculptor spoke like a rough bass, and the owner of a sonorous and a singing voice was a charming artist.

The convicts surrounded the soldiers. They spoke in vain, in a multitude words of different languages. It reminded Babir of a bustling oriental bazaar of Gamon, to which people from all over the world flocked to join a motley and buzzling crowd.

Vashag majestically, as if he were their king, raised his right hand. The conversation subsided. The eyes of the exhausted prisoners were fixed on Vashag and were full of gratitude and hope. Babir smirked - he was always amused by the naive attachment of people to their saviors. He considered such feelings a sign of weakness. Though Vashag saw in them a source of great power, a deep faith and an ineradicable hope for a better future.

He addressed the people:

"You are free! Everyone can go their own way! And let us go our own way!"

"From now on, we have a common path! You gave us freedom!"" murmured the liberated people.

Vashag continued in a more harsh tone:

"Freedom can not be taken away or given! It is either in our hearts or not! So you do not owe us anything, nor do we owe you anything! Go your way!"

"Hear us out, warrior! We can not live on the same land as the Dark Lord. Either his black figure rises and devours us in his shadow, or our songs will sound through the frozen winds and bring back our lands. And you, great warrior, do not be deceived that because your native lands are far away you will be safe. The greed of rulers knows no bounds. And the greed of the Dark Lord is especially nasty. Sooner or later he will send his hordes to your lands, and then there will be nothing you can do to stop him…"

Feeling that his brother is ready to agree with the convict, Babir intervened:

"Listen! We decide for ourselves where we should go and not you!"

"It's a pity that in you there is not as much wisdom as there is strength and courage. For if you look that you'll know! You are not here by chance!"

Babir rested his fists on his hips and sighed. Disputing with stubborn people is difficult..

"Mister Rider take a look!" Elish could hardly stand on his feet, he was crouching under the weight of Babir's bag thrown over his shoulder.

The boy dropped the bag on the ground and 'the stone' rolled out of it. Yes, the very round stone that Babir and Vashag forgot about. The stone, lazily rolling from side to side, rolled up and rested against Vashag's right leg. On it was a pattern, no, the pattern…

The Decision

The pattern looked similar to three flower petals, each of which resembled a drop with a narrow end curved by a whimsical curl. The drops converged in the center and almost touched each other with their narrow ends. Three drops bent along the clockwise direction, which created a sense of their rotation. At the same time, the pattern was very simple and very elegant. Elish liked the pattern unspeakably, and he promised himself that he would certainly weave it … later, when that opportunity would arise.

Neither Babir, nor the warriors, shared Elish's delight. But for Gori and many other convicts, the pattern on the stone fell to taste. Of course, they were artists!

"I thought there would be a skull and bones on the stone or some sword and shield!" Babir was disappointed. "So three petals will plunge the Dark Lord into fear and make him pee himself?"

"It's certainly hard to believe." Vashag said.

People did not disperse, they stood around Vashag. They did not ask for anything, they did not demand anything. However, they mysteriously influenced Vashag. He felt their pain and fear. He was imbued with their hopes and aspirations. Vashag decided to go to the very end!

"We'll split up. Me and Babir will go to visit the Dark Wizard in a cart with stones. We will present the stone with the pattern to him personally and see what happens. The rest of you." He turned to the group "You will go around the country, carrying the pattern as a banner, as a sign of our freedom. Let every village, every town street see it. Draw, write, cut the pattern everywhere so that we can cleanse the earth of this witchcraft. Let it flaunt on the rocks by the roads and on the shields of the soldiers, on the doors of your houses and on your tablecloths!"

Babir looked at his brother with amazed eyes. *"This is insane!"* He repeated to himself. Although in his heart he shared his brother's passion..

THE PATTERN

PART ELEVEN

In which Elish defeats the Dark Lord

Wagon

Stones in the wagon were stacked so that a narrow chamber formed in the middle. At the bottom of the cell there was a trapdoor under the cart. If necessary, they could leave the stone chamber unnoticed. Vashag nicknamed the cart the fortress on wheels, and Babir called it a stone crypt.

The chamber was designed for two - Babir and Vashag. However, Elish flatly refused to part with his guardians. Of course, he cast a tantrum not out of his thirst for adventure, it was all about his strange nature: Elish found it difficult to meet new people, but he was very afraid to part with them when he became attached. As a result, the three of them sat cramped in a tight cell.

The liberated convicts were divided into eleven detachments with one of Vashag's warriors at the head of each of them. The pattern was carefully transferred to everyone and remembered to be remade as best they could later: carvers - wood, glaziers - glass, artists - paper, masons - stone, and blacksmiths - metal. The detachments dispersed. Everyone had to go their own way, so that in seven days they would expand to the walls of the Black City. Going through the villages and towns, it was necessary to collect all those who are able to hold weapons, and bring them, readying for battle, into the lair of the Dark Lord.

Babir, Vashag and Elish climbed into the stone chamber inside the cart. Gori threw a black veil over the stones

with an inscription consisting of the hooked red signs. It was the curse of the Dark Lord and also to anyone who dares to tear off the veil. Gori cleverly climbed into the cart, shouted at the horses, and the wagon shifted from its place.

The path was dangerous, warriors and spies of the Dark Lord were waiting at every step. On the first day the cart was stopped three times by the warriors of the Dark Lord. And it was true, they were so afraid of the red inscription on the veil that they did not approach the wagon and talked with the driver at a decent distance. Vashag and Babir, through the cracks between the stones, watched over and over again, as the warriors of the Dark Lord, saw the inscription from a distance with the curse, the men shivered like fingers in the cold, and fled to the sides. Who would have thought - the curse on the veil protected the enemies of the Dark Lord! At first it surprised them, but then they got used to it. On the third day, Vashag and Babir were completely sure that the guards would not dare to check it on their way into the city.

On the Edge

Overcoming the bottom of the mountain, they saw the capital of the Dark Lord. Through narrow holes between the stones they tried to make out the city as it was difficult. All three climbed out of the trapdoor, exiting the stone fortress.

They stood on the crest of a mountain ridge that crossed the possession of the Dark Lord from north to south. Further down, a road steeply serpentined and disappeared in a dense coniferous forest stretching all the way around the Black City. From the ridge was a beautiful view of the valley. The Black Bity towered on one of the hills in the heart of the valley. The city, with its black walls and thousands of loops resembled a crown planted on the head of a hill. Black smoke rose to the sky with thousands of jets that merged into a giant river of ash and soot, nourished by an immobile black cloud over the city.

"Stop daydreaming! We might get noticed!" Babir showed his usual impatience.

"Well, at least your legs are stretched!" Thought Elish, returning to the stone chamber.

Gori pulled the reins and the cart, creaking the wheels, began descending down the serpentine road.

Downhill the wagon went much faster. It was accelerating more and more. On every bump, it was thrown up. Elish hit his head several times on oak branches that blocked the chamber from falling on them. When the cart rolled to one side or the other, the boy, like a ragdoll, was thrown from side to side.

The wheels creaked so much that it seemed like the cart would fall apart into pieces. Elish curled up and stuffed his ears: the creaking of the wheels was real torture for him. To his relief, after the third turn the road became flatter and the course of the cart slowed.

The serpentine road was a completely deserted place. With the Dark Lord taking over the throne, all evil spirits - from witches to ghouls - ceased to fear and hide, became insolent and step by step captured the surrounding forests and lakes, swamps and fields. Now a journey through the serpentine road would cost a traveller his head. Only the most risky and reckless travelers dared to go down this road, the others lost weeks, but walked around the mountain range.

The cart was so noisy that, no doubt, every terrible creature that inhabited the forest, learned of their presence. Three times in a row monsters blocked the road, but every time the veil with the curse of the Dark Lord forced them to hurry away.

The last obstacle on the way to the Black City was a wide river at the foot of the hill. A stone bridge was built across the river. However, it was too narrow for the cart to cross. Gori turned the wagon north to the left, and they rode on an another, smaller road, along the river's side. At the edge of the forest the roadway turned sharply to the right, towards the river, and went under the water.

On the opposite shore, Gori saw the continuation of the road. He got off the cart and knelt down, as if checking the wheels. He muttered to the comrades hidden in the stone chamber:

"We can't use the bridge to cross the river. So I found a river ford, but I do not know how shallow it is."

"We have no choice and no time!" Answered a choked voice from within.

Gori climbed on the cart and sent the wagon directly into the water. The river bed was very wide, two hundred steps, no less! Who knows what kind of dangers threaten it's dark waters!

"If I move the cart in the river, then the current might turn it on its side! After we enter the water, there will be no turning back! There will not be another chance to change your mind!" Gori warned once more.

"Our minds haven't changed." A voice shouted

"If we don't go, we won't ever have an opportunity like this ever again." Said another.

The Crossing

The horses snorted and refused to enter the river. It's muddy waters frightened the animals. Gori raised the whip, and the stubborn animals obeyed the driver. The horses marched forward, and following them, cutting the water, was the cart. The first half of the river they overcame without any complications. The river was much more shallow than the travelers expected. Movement on the muddy bottom was a difficult test for the horses and the length of the road made them more exhausted.

An unpleasant surprise awaited the travelers ahead. Closer to the opposite shore, the depth of the river began to increase sharply. The stone chamber, which served as a safe hiding place until now, threatened to turn into a crypt filled with water. The level of the water in the chamber kept rising as it moved forward, and soon there was only a small layer of air under its ceiling.

Vashag and Babir desperately pounded against the wall of the chamber and Gori stopped the wagon.

"If the horses make another step, we'll drown here!" Warned Babir.

"We'll leave the chamber and cross the river ourselves, and then we'll plunge back into the cart!" Suggested Vashag.

On the opposite shore appeared a band of warriors of the Dark Lord. They settled on a small hill near the shallows and watched the cart suspiciously.

Gori begun to panic. If they notice the runaway convicts, then they would immediately attack them - the black veil with the curse will not stop them!

"Do not dare show yourself! There are two dozen warriors of the Dark Lord!" Gori turned to Vashag and Babir, pretending to shout at the horses.

"Gori, keep in mind, that if you move even slightly forward, we'll be underwater! If you hesitate in the middle of the river, then we won't have enough time to hold our breaths!" Babir was mostly worried about the boy.

"I understand!" Gori screamed at the horses, and they rushed forward.

The water quickly filled the remaining cavity and all three were completely immersed in the water. Elish was very frightened. Babir laid his hand on his heart; with the other hand making a sign to calm him down. The boy stared into Babir's eyes. He was terrified. But it was this that saved him - Elish froze. Sitting motionless, he did not spend precious gulps of air, which he managed to dial into the lungs before the chamber filled with water. Babir and Vashag were calm, as always. Their faces frozelike stone masks.

Gori whipped the horses mercilessly. The cart moved swiftly forward, then a dull sound was heard - the right front wheel of the cart was wedged against an underwater boulder. The cart rose. It was too heavy to climb over the stone. Gori shouted at the horses, the whip whistled in the air. The animals dragged the cart with all their might, it creaked piteously, but did not move from its place. *The waggon will fall apart!* Thought Goria.

The violent efforts of the driver did not go unnoticed. The soldiers on the shore came closer and stood by the water, making fun of and mocking the unlucky driver.

Elish's eyes begun to turn black. He began to lose consciousness and wanted to open his mouth and breathe in. Babir was faster: he pressed Elish to himself and clamped his nose and mouth shut

"Why are you standing there? Did you turn blind or something? God damn idiots! If the cart turns over, who do you think will be on the bottom looking for and collecting these damned stones?! Or did you forget who they are intended for…" Shouted Gori at the soldiers, but immediately stopped, frightened of his courage.

Gori's call out had an effect. The warriors rushed headlong into the water. Dressed in copper armor, with bulky helmets on their heads, the warriors moved awkwardly and heavily. Trying to move the cart from its place, some dragged it over the sides, others pushed the wheels. Eventually the ill-fated wheel climbed onto the boulder initially blocking its way. The Dark Lords slaves released the cart and began to laugh gaily, but then the cart dangerously tilted to the left side. The driver screamed at the soldiers, showering them with a stream of abuse. The warriors were again on the wagon. While some, stretched like poles, propped the cart from the left side, others on the right side piled on it with all their weight, preventing the wheels from tearing themselves from the bottom.

Gori's eyes continued to follow the soldiers, swarming around the cart, fearing that they would find the chamber inside the masonry.

Elish fainted, his body limp. It was necessary to act urgently! Vashag raised the board that covered the entrance to the cell and left the fortress. He was ready to enter into battle with the wizard's soldiers, just to save the boy. He exited for just a second but the cart jerked forward so sharply that Vashag hardly managed to return back into the chamber. A few seconds passed and the cart moved to the opposite shore.

Water, trickling through the stones, left the chamber. Babir and Vashag made several deep breaths.. Elish was not breathing. He was unconscious, his face was pale, his nails and lips almost black.

"Drive faster!" Babir shouted, completely discarding any caution.

Gori took up the whip. The horses carried the cart up the gentle slope. The warriors of the Black Lord stood in the water, their faces stretched from surprise.

"Talking stones! I've never seen this! Here it is, the Dark Lords sorcerous power!" One of them concluded with an intelligent touch and the others agreed.

Drowned

Gori drove the horses to a pine grove, the nearest place where one could hide. The cart turned off the road and stopped by a big bush.

Babir and Vashag got out from under the cart. Vashag held Elish in his arms. The boy was still unconscious. Laying him on the cold ground, Vashag began to shake the lifeless body.

"Elish! Don't you dare die on us now!" Vashag patted his cheek. On the deadly pale skin of his cheeks were the imprints of his hand. However, the boy did not show any signs of life.

Gori pushed Vashag aside:

"My grandmother is a witch! I saw how she brought people back to life!"

Gori put his fist on Elish's chest, whispered some spells and with another hand struck his chest hard. The rib cage of the boy shuddered from the impact, muddy water flowed from his mouth, but the boy did not come to himself.

"Elish! Open your eyes!" Vashag ordered as if Elish was capricious and pretended to be dead.

Babir silently looked at the desperate attempts to revive the child. He noticed that Elish was still squeezing his last work in his hands, the pattern of the Dark Lord from the branches of the Black Bush. He wove it all the way from the mine, but because of the constant shaking he had to remodel each knot several times. As a result, he finished it only when they reached the river. His fingers convulsively clutched the wicker. It was a pouch for the stone; on it the black branches that Elish had woven formed into three petals.

"His wickerwork is the most precious thing he has! If he is still alive, then ..." Babir grabbed the wicker pattern and pulled it to himself. First, Elish's fingers loosened up, but suddenly the boy groaned deeply and noisily, his eyes wide open. He sat and now properly woken, his hand swung faster than a cobra in the direction of Babir and snatched back the pouch with the pattern. "Give it back! Mine!" Growled Elish.

Babir recoiled and apologetically said: "Calm down! I just wanted to get you back to us!"

Vashag whistled and added: "Well, well, because of your twigs you managed to return from the other side."

Elish wanted to say something in response, but coughed and left the remnants of water from the lungs.

Red Hood

Elish slept through most of the way. The boy had nightmares. Elish saw how his bindweeds burn, how they turn into ashes and turn to smoke. Neither the endless shaking nor the rumbling of the cart could wake him. Babir and Vashag gnawed at themselves for taking him with them, yielding to the whims of the boy.

"It's too late to change anything. He will have to go with us to the end." Guiltily concluded Babir.

"When we get to the castle of the Dark Wizard, Elish should not leave this chamber until everything is over. In this stone fortress nothing will hurt him." Added Vashag.

There was a knock. Gori tapped the flat stone on which he sat three times. They agreed that when they approached the Black City, Gori would give them a signal. The conversation in the chamber ceased.

Five hundred steps remained to the main gate of the Black City. Babir and Vashag tensely watched what was happening around them. The city has become even blacker, and the residents on the streets are even weaker. In the cracks between the stones flashed silhouettes of armed men and woolly monsters in horned helmets with axes. Vashag saw several monsters in iron armor. They were tall and moved on four limbs. The soldiers used them as pack animals and chased them with spears. Babir noticed two more creatures of huge growth with clubs in their hands. Their heads were hiding under their helmets and Babir couldn't understand who they were. "It almost looks like the Dark Wizard is preparing for war." Babir made an already obvious conclusion. Vashag nodded his head in agreement.

Just like all the others during their trip, the guards guarding the main gate did not dare stop the wagon. The travelers passed through under the stone arch. But then they were blocked by a tall, thin man. He wore a dark red robe with a hood, and in his hand a thick golden cane. To Gori's great surprise, he did not turn his back on the curse. It was obvious how his lips moved as he read the letters on the veil.

The man did not give way. "Stop!" He ordered. Taking a step towards the wagon, he continued: "Who are you? Where are you heading?" The man in red did not take his eyes off the poor driver. Gori was afraid of the man in red's determination. Until now, all the warriors and slaves of the Dark Lord had been shaking with fear at the appearance of the cart with a red curse on the black veil.

Babir and Vashag could only watch what was happening out of their stone fortress. *"Maybe they have a password? I did not think about it at all ..."* "At that moment their whole plan seemed childishly naive.

"I'm a driver. I'm leading the cart from the Black Cave." Gori shivered.

"What's in the cart?" Continued the interrogation.

"I do not know! The chief of the mine pulled the veil over the wagon. And what reason should I have to look at something the boss places. Foreign secrets are an unbearable burden for a small person like me."

The man in the red cane lifted the veil, walked around the wagon and looked suspiciously at it. "Turn it around!" He shouted.

"The plan failed!" Babir prepared for the final battle.

"It was all for naught!" Vashag looked guiltily at Elish.

Gori swallowed his saliva and turned the cart back.

Elish woke up, but he was afraid to open his eyes. His heart sank to pain. He clearly felt the danger. It came from the strange person outside. The boy was seized with even greater fear than when he was alone with the Black Bush, and even more than at the crossing. The whole city was permeated, like an infection, with fear. Fear, like a stink, penetrated into the stone chamber. Elish was frightened for his twigs, he imagined that his braided handicrafts were engulfed by a ruthless flame. Elish embraced them and pressed it to his chest.

Vashag noticed that the pattern on the stone began to glow slightly. He touched it and felt the his fear diminish. Vashag gestured to Elish and laid his hand on the stone. The boy calmed down. Fear vanished, as if the stone had swallowed him. Even the man in red did not seem so terrible anymore.

When the cart drove out of the city gates, the man in red shook his cane and ordered the driver to follow him. They turned left and headed along the fortress wall, alongside a weedy narrow path.

The Tunnel

The man in red stopped at the entrance to a tunnel that led beneath the fortification of the wall. The lights of the rare torches on the walls barely illuminated him. The tunnel went straight, without turns - at first it came down, and then it rose abruptly.

The man in the red threw back his hood and Gori screamed when he saw his face. In fact, it was not a face, but a skull, covered with white skin, without wrinkles or blemishes. The man in red, without warning, hit Gori unconscious with his cane and the driver dropped from the cart. The man in red took the horse by the bridle and led the cart into the tunnel. He lashed the poor animals and the horses rushed down the tunnel, carrying the cart behind them. Hooves clinked loudly on the floor paved with stones. The burning lights on the walls rushed past the stone chamber, casting curves of light on its walls and the faces sitting inside it.

The dirty wastewater flooded the middle of the tunnel due to the fact that it was lower than the beginning and end. The horses carried the cart, and its wheels sprayed water, leaving mud stains on the walls.

Giants on the Walls

The tunnel opened into a spacious hall. The room was a square. The ceiling disappeared in the dark; light from the oil lamps, fixed on the walls, were not enough to illuminate the vault of the hall.

In addition to the gaping exit from the tunnel, there was another small door in the opposite corner. On the walls Vashag saw inscriptions similar to those that were inscribed on the coverlet. On each of the four walls there were painted white portraits of giants. They stood with their legs wide apart and arms crossed. The giants had no faces - a bald head with just ears on the sides, without eyes, mouth or nose. "Blind watchmen?" Babir asked. Vashag only spread his hands.

The travelers did not leave the fortress on wheels, waiting for the Dark Lord to appear. But the hall remained empty, and the painted giants were motionless.

At midnight the door opened and a shadow slipped into the hall. It was him. The Dark Lord, having finished his pile of state affairs,he left the throne room and walked into the square hall all alone, where he was waiting for another cart with stones from the Black Cave. Waiting until the man in red stepped through the door and it locked behind him on a strong wooden bolt, the Dark Lord stepped wearily into the middle of the hall.

Nobody in the Black City could imagine what was happening under the city square. Even the man in red did not really know what was going on at the other end of the tunnel and where the dozens of carts with stones go. The Dark Lord kept in secret the story of the stone with the pattern. If anyone finds out what the pattern is on the stone, then his dark power will come to an end! After all, there will always be someone who dares to overthrow the Dark Lord himself from the throne and take his place. All the carts were delivered to the square room, and he himself dismantled the stones, or so the others thought. Of course, the sorcerer did not intend to disassemble thousands of stones. And not only out of laziness or because of their severity. He was afraid that with the next wagon he would find 'the stone', on which the very pattern was traced on. The Dark Lord created four blind monsters with the power of black magic, who dismantled the stones. Give them the stone with the pattern and they would not see it and therefore would not be frightened. And if they don't not see it - they would not remember. And if they don't remember it - they would not spill the secret.

It was the Dark Lord's genius masterpiece.

Once in the hall, the Dark Lord felt the tension in the air. A chill ran through his skin. The sorcerer was sure that the cart arrived, that had 'the stone'. He rejoiced. At last he will get rid of the stone that made him vulnerable, humiliatingly weak. The stone was closer than ever - a little more and the pattern will disappear forever!

With the air of a triumphant conqueror, the sorcerer raised his hands and began to read the spells in a language understood only by him.

Neither Vashag nor Babir saw the Dark Lord. They only heard the sound of the spells that reached the cart in the empty hall. But they could see as the sorcerer's spell awakens the giants painted on the wall. The stones around the painted giants began to radiate a flickering bluish light. The lines on the wall moved, then the wall swelled, and in a moment the giants separated themselves from the painting, as if rock golems emerging from molten lava.

The blind giants, stepping heavily, moved away from the walls. Two of them headed to the far corner of the room, where two large stone slabs stood, one on top of the other. Each of the slabs was a cylinder, tall as a human and as wide as two. Logs stuck out from the top slab, inserted inside a hollowed out pillar. The eyeless giants, finding the logs, pushed on them. With a gnash, the top plate began to spin, grinding everything that remained between the two plates. Elish clamped his ears.

"Huge millstones! They will blast any stone into dust!" Babir guessed.

Two other giants approached the cart. One of them pulled the veil and threw it to the floor, ignoring the curse inscribed on it. Leaning down, he took in his palm several stones, lying on top. Another giant followed his example. They carried the stones to the rotating millstones and lowered them into the hole in the middle of the upper plate. Stones rolled down the chute that passed through the top plate. The millstones grinded the stones like grain. While some giants were turning the millstones, the other two returned to the cart for a new portion of stones. The first of the giants grabbed a handful, leaving the wooded foundation in which the travelers sat, without a roof. The second bent over the cart. He ran his hand directly into the wooded foundations. The blind giant did not see the people lurking in the cart. Elish screamed. The giant stopped in surprise. Babir had no choice - he stood up to his full height and with all his might sliced the giant's neck twice with his sword. He wrapped his fingers around his bleeding neck with both hands, groaning. It started swaying and then fell down dead.

The millstone suddenly stopped. The other three giants turned to the cart.

"Some uninvited guests arrived with the stone!" Now the Black Lord was certain that the stone was here.

The giants, stamping their feet, were advancing on the wagon.

"We must get out of the cart! Otherwise, we will be turned into powder together with it in the millstones!" Vashag bared his sword.

"Take the stone! I'll distract the giants, and you should try to attack the sorcerer with it." Babir replied.

"What should I do?" Elish asked in panic.

"The tunnel will lead you out of the city walls. Wait for us there! Soon my troop will arrive and get us out." Vashag hoped that at least the boy would survive.

As soon as they jumped out of the stone chamber, one of the giants kicked the cart with his foot. It shattered into splinters, and stones rolled on the floor.

The Stone

He did not have to explain to Elish twice, taking his handicrafts under his arm, the boy tossed himself down the tunnel. Babir remained at the broken cart. "And what should I do with the giants?" The warrior looked doubtfully at the sword. He measured the giants with one look: "It will not be easy to reach the neck!".

Vashag lay on the floor under the wreckage of the wagon. When the giant drove their foot into it, the stones from the overturned cart fled violently across the hall. One hefty stone hit Vashaag in the leg, and he fell, slightly injured, on the floor. Vashag held the stone with the pattern in his hands, but his blade was broken.

Babir ran and jumped on the giant's belly, who smashed the cart with his foot. He raised his sword and lowered it to the neck of the giant. The giant managed to put down his head before Babir could pierce anything. The sword hit the top of his hard head, slid to the right and crashed into the shoulder. The blind giant waved his hands, as if fighting off a bee swarm. One blow hit Babir on the back and he flew down from his stomach, rolled around and crashed into a column ... No, it was not a column, but a swollen foot of another giant. The second giant grabbed Babir with both hands.

Vashag, waking up, hurried to the aid of his brother. He repeatedly thrust the broken blade into the giant's leg. But the giant did not feel pain. He squeezed Babir so that his human bones cracked. Babir lost consciousness, and the heavy sword slipped from his weakened hands. The sword flew with the point down and yet it didn't touch the ground - Vashag caught the sword in the air. He crouched down like a lynx before a jump, and rushed upwards, onto the giant's back. A moment later, his sword went down the hilt into the flesh of the giant, just where the ugly head began to form from it's formless body. The second giant sank and fell to the floor.

Vashar took his sword out of the giant's carcass and ran to his brother. Babir had already risen and rubbed his injured sides, his eyes still on the giants advancing on them.

"We have one sword for two warriors!" Vashag stretched the hilt of his sword towards Babir, as the tradition dictated.

"One sword for two giants! Were in a bit of a sticky situation aren't we."

"They are blind! They can not catch us!"

The Dark Lord laughed so loudly that the laughter echoed through the hall and raised some winged creatures in the air under the roof. Babir and Vashag heard the clapping of wings at the top, but in the dark they could not see anything.

The Dark Lord did not dare to approach Babir and Vashag because of the fear of the pattern on the stone. He stood consumed with hatred for the Great Magician, who created the magic pattern, for the stone and for the two insolent ones who challenged him.

The giants shifted their feet awkwardly. At each step they kicked the stones lying on the floor, which, striking each other, scattered around the hall. The brothers retreated back. Babir, swiftly spinning with his sword, kneaded his muscles.

"We can't attack from the front!" Babir stopped.

"Do you suggest passing the sword to each other and taking turns fighting them?" Vashag deftly dodged a stone, on which the giant drove his foot.

"I'm not suggesting anything. Nothing at all. We run to them. While the giants will be busy with me." Babir put the sword in front of him, "You will run between them."

"A very interesting solution!" Vashag answered with a puzzled expression.

Face to Face

Babir rushed at the giants. He slashed the left side of the one that stood closer. Babir dodged the retaliatory strike that followed and jumped to the second giant and jabbed it with the tip of the sword in it's big toe. Jumping back, he did not calculate the distance and crashed into the giant standing behind him. Babir did not fall and still on his feet, but he was between two bloodthirsty giants.

"Hurry!" Babir shouted at Vashag, still standing.

Vashag grabbed the stone with his hands and rushed forward. He contrived to slip between the giants. Vashag sped directly towards the Dark Lord. He lifted the stone over his head and revealed the pattern to the Dark Lord. The stone became heavier than it was before. The Dark Lord backed away. He trembled with fear.

"You have nowhere to run!" Vashag gave the wizard an ultimatum.

The Dark Lord's life was retreated. His eyes burned with impotent rage. The path to the door through which the Dark Lord came from was cut off. The sorcerer went to the second remaining exit - the tunnel.

The stone became prohibitively heavy in the presence of the Dark Lord. And it continued to grow heavy as it approached the sorcerer. Vashag begun panting, sweat streamed down his back. With trembling hands, he tried to hold the stone over his head: *I'll crush the accursed sorcerer! Another twenty steps, and this stone will be on his head!*

"Vashag! Hurry!" Shouted Babir.

Vashag was unable to turn around. His strength was at an end - the stone sucked it out of him. If Vashag looked back, he would have seen that the third giant was lying dead on the floor, but the latter had caught Babir with it's huge arms and like a sponge, squeezed him - just like the millstones grinding at the rock.

The Dark Lord sank to the floor and begun chanting up a new spell.

"It will not help you! You and your magic are powerless before the sight of the pattern!" Only a couple of steps separated Vashag from the sorcerer crouching on the floor. "Your charms dissipate at the appearance of its magnificence."

The sorcerer continued to chant the spells, until a rumble was heard from under the roof of the hall, in the darkness among the rafters. The Dark Lord jumped up and began to rotate his staff over his head. Black clouds begun forming above them in the dark. They tore off the rafters and circled the room. Until the cloud became like a cartwheel covered in soot, gradually descending on the ones below.

Once it came down far enough, it's composition can be seen in the light, Vashag saw that it was in fact not a black cloud, but a swarm of hungry bats.

"The pattern has no power over those who are blind!" The Dark Lord laughed angrily.

The clouds of bats descended from under the arch, silently circling. In a moment, the bats filled the space between Vashag and the Dark Lord. The sorcerer disappeared into the living stream of creatures.

The flow of bats rushed into a ring around Vashag. Their flight speed increasing. The stream moved faster and faster, the ring became denser and denser. Vashag felt dizzy. Everything swam before his eyes. Vashag felt that he was losing consciousness. He threw the stone using his last bit of strength to the place where the sorcerer had just stood. The stone flew through the close rows of bats and landed on the sorcerer. The Dark Lord whimpered in pain and the stone rolled into the tunnel. The shroud of bats again closed and hid the Dark Lord from Vashag's eyes. Taking advantage of the fact that Vashag does not see him, the sorcerer, overcoming the pain, crawled towards the tunnel.

Vashag did not fend off the hordes of flying creatures - he simply did not have the strength. He only covered his face with his hands. Bats painfully bit him, each time tearing away a piece of human flesh.

Vashag cowered on the ground. Bats began to drum on his back. The chain mail turned into pathetic rags; the small sharp teeth of the flying creatures penetrated into the slots. Vashag could not fight back - the stone took any strength he had left.

But someone grabbed and dragged him by the collar. Vashag raised his head and met his gaze with his brother.

"Get up! We need to get to the millstone!" Shouted Babir. "You won't be able to fend against them for long!"

Like a blizzard or a sandstorm the clouds of flying predators enveloped them. Babir stretched his shoulder out to Vashag. They slowly crawled, Babir shielding his injured brother from the bat's biting frenzy. They headed towards the large millstones.

Once they reached them, Babir helped his brother to scramble to the top plate. The gutter was wide enough, and they both hid in it. Babir put up his shield and covered them both. The bats were drumming on it's forged hardness, but it's unbreakable structure was too hard for them.

The bats took a few minutes to recover from the giants flesh, who's bones was the only thing that remained. Four giants have kindled their appetite. The cloud of the winged bloodsuckers gathered at the closed door - because from it came the smell of human blood. The doors were heavy and solidly built, but, as they say, the water grinds the stone. Thousands of bats crashed into the door and flew to the side only to return again and again. Blow after blow they shook the door...

Another cloud gathered at the entrance to the tunnel. The bats looked like swarming bees. The Dark Lord, who woke up the little monsters, was now himself the hostage. The sorcerer held the staff in his arms outstretched in front of him. The staff sparkled, emitting waves of bright light. The sorcerer recited his incantations - the only thing that held back the storm of the winged bloodsuckers. The sorcerer knew that the wooden doors in the opposite end of the hall would not last long, and it would be worthwhile to crawl towards the other exit, as this living stream of death would go into the door that opens. "It will definitely be a certain death for anyone who gets in their way... It's a pity, I will lose many slaves!" The sorcerer weighed his options. "But it doesn't matter! The important thing is that I have the stone!"

Vashag was bleeding. He kept repeating: "Babir, we must find the boy! It's not good for us to sit here." Babir raised his shield and a couple of bats flew into the gap. With his fist Babir smeared them one by one against the wall of the gutter. "How do we get to him?!" Exclaimed Babir in frustration.

Flying Monsters

It was clear that the bats were attracted to both the door and the people inside the room.

So when light from the sorcerer spell had dimmed, the bats suddenly rushed down the tunnel after the wizard, but three or four steps before they reached the Dark Lord, the bats struck against the magical invisible shield created by the sorcerer's spells. The invisible barrier was stronger than damask steel.

The Dark Wizard concentrated all his energy on the little bloodsuckers who were trying to break through the wizard's barrier. If he stopped to relax for even a second the stream of bats will rush along the tunnel, leaving the sorcerer as a pile of gnawed bones. But more than their sharp teeth, the Dark Wizard was troubled by the fate of the stone with the pattern. Thoughts of the Dark Lord were at the same time focusing here in the tunnel and in the hall where he made a mistake and missed the stone. "No one should know about the pattern, and anyone who finds out what it looks like must die!" The sorcerer groped around the tunnel with his inner eye and was looking for it between the scattered stones - a stone with the hated pattern of three petals. The sorcerer was so absorbed in the search for the stone that he did not hear the timid steps behind him. It was Elish.

The boy, as Vashag ordered him, ran to the tunnel, but, reaching the middle of the tunnel, stood at the edge of the water that had flooded it. He stood, and then turned back towards the hall, never venturing into the water after what happend hours earlier. Elish's path was blocked by a figure of a man in black robes with a staff in his hand. The man stood with his back to him. In the cold, looking inside, and the wild fear that gripped him. Elish realized that this is the Dark Lord himself. Elish pressed himself against the wall of the tunnel and crouched down, afraid to be seen. Out of this fear he put the bag across his face with a picture of a pattern that he wove all the way from the Black Cave. The silhouette of the sorcerer blackened against the bright blue light emanating from his staff. Further along the corridor, something unimaginable was happening: countless flocks of bats rushed before the sorcerer, until they struck against the invisible shield and fell at his feet.

The Scramble

Vashag gathered his strength and pushing Babir away, climbed out of the gutter. "I will not allow these damned bloodsuckers to hurt the boy!" Vashag ran to the tunnel and landed in the thick of the bats swarming at the entrance. Babir followed his brother, but lost sight of him in the hall full of the volatile creatures.

Babir shouted so fiercely that he could easily be mistaken for a angry lion or a mad bull and the bats in the air began to thin out! They disappeared from the hall like water running out from a cracked jar. Babir became proud, attributing their disappearance to his menacing cry. But soon he saw what was the real reason: the wooden doors collapsed, unable to withstand the violent storm. Now the bats rushed down the corridors and galleries of the Dark Lord's castle, promising an agonizing death to its inhabitants. The winged bloodsuckers demanded the continuation of their feast, and nothing could stop them.

Babir found Vashag lying unconscious at the entrance to the tunnel. Vicious bats flew past Babir and disappeared in the doorway in the opposite end of the hall. The screams coming from the castle testified that the bloody feast was in full swing.

Babir grabbed his brother by the shoulders and lifted him. Vashag did not move. Tears manifested in Babir's eyes, his heart begging to sink

In the tunnel appeared the Dark Lord, hunched over. Noticing Babir, the sorcerer cried out. He did not expect that after the bloody storm caused by the mad bats, there will be anyone alive in the hall.

Babir attacked the sorcerer. The Dark Lord tried to dodge, but slipped on the wet paving stones and fell flat on the floor. Babir attacked with the sword. The Dark Lord managed to put forth his staff. The point of the sword stopped near the heart of the sorcerer.

In an honest duel with a real warrior, the Dark Lord had no chance, but with his magic tricks he counterbalanced their strengths. The Dark Lord uttered a spell, and Babir's blade glowed white-hot so that the hilt of the sword caught fire. Babir released his sword and lowered his burned hands into a puddle on the floor. The smell of burning flesh hung in the air.

The Dark Lord raised his heavy staff over his head. The knob at the end of the staff was charged with short white lightning bolts.

"Fools, you yourself have brought me what I've been looking for for many years! A stone with the pattern is the only thing that could get in my way! You could of asked for a reward - gold, land, whatever! But no! Today the pattern will be shattered to oblivion forever! And everyone who saw it will follow! There is no more damned magicians to draw another pattern!"

The sorcerer was about to lower his staff on the warrior's head.

Babir grabbed the sorcerer by the waist and pushed him to the floor. Both rolled along the tunnel. The staff fell next to Babir's sword, hissing and smoking from touching a puddle. Two men clung each others throats and each hoped to strangle the other. They rolled down the tunnel until they hit the water. The sorcerer twisted and sat on Babir. Babir remained submerged. Through the dirty water he could see the sorcerer leaning over him, his red eyes burning with hatred. Babir was exhausted, his hands fell. *What an inglorious end ...* The thought flashed through his mind one final time.

Braided Pattern

The Dark Lord, feeling that his rival is weakening, squeezed his throat even more. "Die! Ten ... Nine ... Do not resist ... Eight ... Seven ... A little more and it will be over ... Six ... Five ... " The sorcerer waited for the heart of his victim to stop beating.

Then a little boy interfered, who was behind him all the time. Elish collected the remnants of his courage and crept behind the sorcerer. All the way from the Black Cave, he wove a bag with the pattern, the same as on the stone. He wove a cover for the stone, but the stone was lost among thousands of others. Elish stepped completely inaudible but still feared that his heart was beating too loudly and the sorcerer would hear him. Standing just behind the Dark Lord, the boy hit him on the head with the bag. The pattern on the bag began to glow with a weak warm light. The Dark Lord groaned and froze. Elish pushed the sorcerer off Babir's body and lifted the warrior's head from the water.

"Mister Babir! Are you alive? I still have to go home! You promised ..." Elish mumbled.

Babir opened his eyes, his body shuddered. He shot out the water, sat and looked around, not understanding what was going on.

Ghost or Man

Babir froze motionless, trying to remember what had happened.

"Elish? You were told to wait outside!" Babir rebuked the boy.

"How could I pass through the tunnel if the passage was flooded with water?! I don't really feel like drowning a second time!" Elish was offended.

"And where is the wizard?" Babir felt guilty for having offended Elish, but to apologize to the child was against his rules.

The boy pointed to the frozen wizard with a bag on his head.

"How did you know to put a patterned bag on his head?" Babir caught himself thinking that he was sucking up to the boy.

"Guessed? Honestly, I didn't even have time to think. I only had the bag in my hand and nothing else…" Said Elish, frowning.

The Dark Lord lay in the water with a bag on his head. Babir unexpectedly noticed how beautifully the red and orange flower petals shone on the bag. Convinced that the sorcerer can not escape, Babir ran to his brother.

However, Vashag had disappeared. On the spot where Babir left his wounded brother, only traces of blood remained. "Did the flying monster not even leave his bones!" From this bitter thought the warrior's heart contracted even more.

But Elish's sharp-sighted eye saw the pale silhouette of Vashag in the dim light .

"Mister Rider!" Elish called.

Vashag, moving his legs with difficulty, wandered among the scattered stones at the far end of the hall. Pale from the loss of blood, he was more like a cemetery ghost than a living person.

"Vashag! Brother!" Tears welled in Babir's eyes from joy.

Vashag did not hear him - he was completely absorbed in the search for the stone. When Babir and Elish came to him, he had just found the stone with the pattern. Vashag sat down on one knee and raised the stone with both hands. To his amazement, the stone was light, as on the day they found it at the bottom of the cave.

BACK HOME

THE FINAL PART

*In which the Dark Lord is returned to the cave,
the Khan's troops are sent to their families and Elish goes home*

Back to the Surface

Babir tied the Dark Wizard with his belt. Overcoming the water that accumulated in the middle of the tunnel, it was easy - it was knee-deep. However, Elish still resisted entering the water. He was persuaded for a long time, but the obstinate boy disagreed. Babir had to take on both of them: a bound sorcerer, and a boy afraid of water. He could not help his brother, because he could barely drag his own feet.

Outside, by the fortress wall, there was nobody. The man in red disappeared without a trace and Gori was nowhere to be seen either.

The travelers followed the road along the fortress wall to the main gate of the city. People came from the whole valley to the gate. The soldiers from Vashag's troop carried out their order correctly. People, armed with pitchforks and axes, hoes and hammers, came here to fight the Dark Lord and his army. The crowd was loud and angry, but all of them had the pattern of three petals on their shirts. The pattern was on wooden shields and even on the bow of a battering ram.

The city was in turmoil. Clouds of bats shot out of the castle of the Dark Lord remainders of his warriors jumped out of the windows and doors of the castle. Flocks of bats bursting out, sowing panic among the citizens of the Black City.

Then Gori ran up to the travelers. Seeing his liberators, he embraced them. Gori was very excited by what he saw. Seeing the bound sorcerer at Babir's feet, Gori blurted out:

"We must judge and punish him!"

"The Great Magician has already condemned the Dark Wizard for an eternal stay in the Black Cave! We will return him there!"

Gori shifted from foot to foot, examining the once mighty and great, now wretched and powerless.

"You must lead us to storm the Black City!" Gori turned to Vashag.

"It would be a great honor for me. But one of you must lead the fight! Find the hero among you, and let him go forward!" Answered Vashag.

"You could become our king!" Gori exclaimed.

"No. Your king is also among you. Find him! You can! It's time for us to go!" Interposed Babir.

"Find the green ribbon with the emblem of our Khan in the castle. This is our offer of peace and friendship. Put the ribbon on the coat of arms of Itil and send it to the 'City-by-the-Sea'. We will tie it with a triple knot on the sacred Oath Tree as ours and yours promise of peace." Vashag did not forget why he was sent to the north.

In the end, Gori embraced Babir and Vashag once more, patted the ruffled hair of Elish and ran to the city gates, where the siege was about to begin.

Riding in two groups, Vashag's troop went along the mountain road back to the Black Cave. When they climbed the serpentine road, the could hear that the people began the assault. When the travelers reached the ridge, the city was completely in the hands of the people - on the fortress walls, flags with the pattern of the three petals were hung.

The Shaft

Babir and Vashag brought the Dark Wizard to the Black Cave to re-imprison him in the magnificent palace belonging to the strange creature called Echo. Around the cave, except for crows and the hungry wolves, there was no one. The horses unharnessed, the group occupied the lodge.

Babir and Vashag were thoroughly prepared to immerse themselves in the mine. They were stocked with food and water, took swords and rope ladders, and - most importantly - torches and flint. The brothers did not want to repeat the horrors of wandering around the cave in the pitch darkness, tripping over and hitting their heads against walls.

Elish was begging for Babir 's and then Vashag's permission to go down with them to the mine, the whole way. Babir surrendered first. "Well aren't you a nagging little brat! Did you lose a twig in this musty cave or something?!" The warrior was indignant, but in order to stop the stubborn boy, he agreed. "Why do you need to go down into the cave?" Vashag was surprised, but too, unable to bear the nagging boy, agreed to take him down. Elish also kept the secret the reason why he wanted to once again enter the terrible dungeon.

Descending in to the mine, Babir and Vashag set fire to the torches. The light lit up the interior of the cave and an ominous picture appeared before the travelers. Babir and Vashag first saw the place that served as the gloomy prison for them and for thousands of other captives of the Dark Wizard.

Vashag and Elish walked in front, and Babir, who was carrying the sorcerer with a bag on his head, closed the formation. The cave was empty - all the prisoners left it, all except for Echo. On the walls here, there were scratched names: convicts were afraid that they would not return home, and wrote their names on the walls in the hope that they will have at least some memory. Still on the walls were columns of dashes: the people imprisoned in the cave counted the days spent here. Vashag pointed to a stove between two large stones. Above it was written "Vashag and the eleven." And below - even columns, like troops on a parade.

"Stop!" Commanded Vashag, who was ahead. There was no further passage. The whole corridor was flooded with branches of the Black Bush, which grew during their absence. It's branches stretched menacingly toward the intruders and stood tensely.

"I know another way around!" Vashag led the companions to another corridor. However, there also waited thickets of the Black Bush. The bush completely blocked the passage.

"We're wasting our time!" Exclaimed the annoyed Babir.

Elish approached the bush and said in a reconciling tone:

"Do not be afraid of it. It's not bad at all."

The bush, having heard the speech of the boy, calmed down, its branches submissively sank to the ground and the passage opened. Vashag and Babir, trying not to step on the branches of the bush, passed through the overgrown thickets. The boy let them go forward, and he lingered among the powerful branches that enveloped the corridor.

"I'll wait for you here. I need to talk with my friend." Elish said.

This was the reason why he went down into the awful cave!

Babir did not have time to object. The branches rose into the air and covered Elish.

"Do not worry. I'm safe here. Get me on the way back." Came Elish's voice from the thicket of the Black Bush.

There was no choice, they had to move on.

Descent to the bottom of the cave was not very difficult - with fire in their hands they moved quickly. Elish's wicker dolls were still pointing the way to the underground palace of the insane Echo.

The travelers knew the steps and turns, they recognized smells and sounds. But everything was a little different. The light of burning torches tore off the veil of mystery and fear from the darkness of the cave.

After traversing the twisting underground passages they reached the hall from which they last time fell from into the palace of Echo. Wizened with experience, they cautiously approached and, bending over the hole, called the owner of the underground palace:

"Echo-oh-oh! We brought to you an old friend!"

On the rope, like a large doll, they lowered the sorcerer down.

"I'm sure you will not be bored together!" Added Vashag.

"Like two scorpions in a jar!" Babir laughed.

"Perfect!" Echo was interested. "Let's see who will brighten up my loneliness."

Echo removed the bag with the pattern from the head of the Dark Wizard.

The creaky voice of the sorcerer cut through the silence:

"I'll destroy you all! I'll turn you into miserable mice!"

Echo ran to one side:

"How?! It's ..." Echo paused. "The Dark Lord!"

It was impossible to understand whether he was happy or, on the contrary, annoyed. But the Dark Wizard was unequivocally not happy.

"It would be better if you buried me alive, by myself! So I don't have to listen to his endless chatter until the end of time!" The sorcerer screamed in despair.

"Is your highness still nervous?" Echo began, "do not worry soon the anger will pass. Here, in my magnificent palace, you will find peace ..."

"Is it me or do they get along pretty well!" Babir said with mockery.

"I'm not staying here! I got out of this cave once and I'll do it again!" The sorcerer did not calm down.

"Yet it seem like you're forgetting something, wizard. Probably the sack on your head is to blame. First, your capital was returned to its rightful owners. And secondly, the pattern you love has spread all across the land - from here to the Black City. This cave is the only place where there is no pattern! In this pleasant company, years will fly by like a short night…" Babir laughed.

"It's a pity we won't get to see the palace! Is it as beautiful as Echo praises it to be?" Vashag thought.

Moving from one woven doll to another, the brothers returned back. Babir collected the dolls in a large bag so that no one else found a way to the underground palace and did not release the Dark Wizard.

When they got to the Black Bush, it lowered the branches, politely passing the guests through the formed passage. Elish was waiting for them. His mood was high. True, he never told Babir and Vashag about what he was whispering with the Black Bush while they were at the bottom of the cave.

On their way out of the cave Vashag looked back at where the Bush was. "If this man-eating bush does not scare men from going down into these caves. I don't know what will." He thought, knowing that the Dark Wizards imprisonment was sure to be endless.

Thousands of Lives for One - Love

By the end of the fifth week, the group reached the Iron Gates. Yalov was the first to see the fortress walls. He joyfully screamed like a sailor on a mast, who, after a grueling voyage, first saw the long-awaited land in the distance.

"Well, home sweet home." Babir imagined how he would roast a good lamb and roll a feast with his warriors.

"Babir, we are too late." Vashag pointed out the tents with the banners of the great Khan at the fortress walls. "The Khan is going to war with the north."

"He did not leave the land's limits. There is still time to return the troops to the barracks!" Babir spurred his horse.

The brothers trotted the horses to the Khan's headquarters, leaving Elish with the rest of the men far behind.

Approaching the camp, the horses slowed down. The guard ordered them to stop:

"Stop! Get down from the horses and state your names!"

Vashag said:

"Peace be with you, Keshish! You did not recognize me again. Do not delay me, for I hasten to see the ruler."

The guard smiled at Vashag.

"And peace to you too! I dare not detain you. You again are all covered in dirt. More like a drifter than a minister's son. You need to go into the hamam. Although not sure if there is a one nearby."

The horsemen dismounted and, having passed through the camp, approached the Khan's tent. The tent of the ruler was no different from the tents of other soldiers, only an flag on the vertex of the tent portrayed the high position of their master. The luxury that was so loved in the 'City-by-the-Sea,' had no place in a camp like this. "Luxury in a campaign - is extra load for the horses" liked to repeat the practical Khan.

The Khan sat on the carpet and played chess with the minister on a long pillow across from him. Vashag did not interfere with their game. He quickly assessed the situation on the chessboard: the black pieces are doomed. The Khan made a move. Convinced that he had made the right move, he rose vigorously to his feet and embraced Vashag. Vashag respectfully bowed to his father and turned to the Khan:

"We have fulfilled your order, great Khan! The North will not be our enemy!"

"Did the Dark Lord accept our gifts and good intentions?"

"No great Khan. But the people of the north have accepted our good intentions."

"And what about their master, the Dark Lord?"

"He did not appreciate your generosity. And the people questioned his wisdom."

The Khan raised his eyebrows.

"Do they have a new king?"

"Yes, great Khan."

"Is the new king our enemy?"

"No, friend. We have many friends in the north."

"You've become very close to strangers, Vashag. It happens every time you wander for a long time in a foreign land."

"Maybe. But now the north is not our enemy."

The Khan sat down in his chair. His gaze was fixed on the chessboard. It seemed that he was considering the next move in the chess game.

"You're right, Vashag. A good neighbor is better than a bad relative. I let it be. And where is your brother Babir?"

"Waiting outside."

"Tell him to enter."

Babir went inside.

"How many people do you need to keep the northern border safe?" Asked the Khan to Babir.

"Those that already exist, and a dozen more."

"Let it be so."

When the brothers left the tent, the Khan remembered about Elish:

"How's the boy that made the harness? He is a skilled master. I hope he's back with you?"

"Yes. He gave you a present."

Vashag held out a sack with a pattern.

"He wove that bag. There is the stone in it that plunged the Dark Lord to his defeat."

Khan took a gold dagger from his scabbard:

"Tell the boy. A gift from the Khan! To save such a boy, it is not a pity to sacrifice a thousand soldiers, including me and the minister!"

"Thousands of lives for one - love." Vashag spoke the third of the calligraphy, depicted above the door in the palace of the ruler.

The Familiar Barn

Babir took the patrol and stayed with his men at the Iron Gate. Vashag returned his men back to their homes, and at last, took Elish to his.

Elish was greeted by boys in the village, yes, the same ones who liked to mock him. Seeing Elish riding on a noble horse, accompanied by a noble warrior, the boys bowed and gave way.

They rode until they reached the very house, he was greeted by the ecstatic views of his neighbours. People poured out onto the street and lined up along the road, talking excitedly.

Arriving at Elish's house, Vashag called the owner. Elish's father shed tears when he met his son.

"Peace to you. Did you recognise me?" Vashag turned to him.

"Peace to you too. Yes, of course sir. You honored us and dined with us at the lake where I was fishing."

"Correct. The great Khan sends you a greeting and his blessing. Know that your son saved us from great misfortune. As a token of gratitude, the Khan sent you gifts. And ten more gold each month until the day Elish grows into a man. In spring and early autumn I will bring its contents. After he's matured, he will be free to enter the service of the Khan or live a free life. Until then, do not obstruct him, he is free to choose his classes: he can weave, how much he wants, what he wants and for whom he wants to! This is the will of the great Khan."

Vashag embraced the boy, kissed him on the forehead and said:

"You can become a great master if you want. You can, but you don't have to. Remember, you are free to do whatever you need to do. I have a gift for you."

Vashag gave him the magic postal dove.

"If you need a sharp blade or a pair of strong fists, whisper my name or my brother's name to the bird. The dove will tell us that you need help. Just do not forget to feed her!" said Vashag as his farewell.

Vashag left. And the whole village ran to honor the hero. The father got a sheep for this occasion. The mother laid the table. The guests congratulated their father on his son's return, greeted his son, hugged them both. And everyone considered it their duty to shake Elish's hand and to shave the sheep of it's curly coat. Elish patiently shrugged everything that was happening to the side. Waiting for the evening when the guests would disperse.

At dusk, the house was empty. The father enthusiastically talked with Elish's uncles. The mother and sister left the table.

Elish furtively went to his barn. Here he finally felt at home. He took off his glove. Golden nails glittered in the twilight. He was no longer afraid of the dark. Even learned how to weave in it.

Elish took out of his pocket the seeds of the Black Bush. It was because of them that he climbed into the cave a second time. He also asked the Black Bush about magical wickering. But that's a story for another day.

Until then, Elish planted the seeds in the center of the barn and sat waiting, reflecting on all that had happened, unaware that his story - was far from over.

Extra Chapter by Translator: **Babir's Revenge.**

Babir stood calmly in his quarters, looking out of the window towards the northern lands. He was reflecting on all that had happened, just like Elish had done far away.

Just as he was scrolling through the memories of his journey, something suddenly came to light.

He turned around and smiled with a mischievously evil grin.

Without telling you what he had remembered, all I can say for sure is that whoever he was visiting was about to get into a lot of trouble.

He walked down the stairs and through the grand hall, waving at his men who had just woke up from a night of drinking and eating. Half of them collapsed on the floor from the strong beverages that were served. He walked through the courtyard covered in melting snow, melting from the sun the spring was about to bring. He walked up the stone stairs that lead up to the wall facing the south and looked around. His eyes captured it's target and Babir smiled once more, readying himself for what's about to happen.

"Good Morning, you must be the vice-chief guard, how are things looking out there!"

The guard was sleepy and quiet unresponsive, playing carelessly with his blade and all that came out of his mouth was-

"Guuahhood.."

Babir grabbed the guard by the shoulder and turned him towards himself. He raised his hand and slapped the guard hard across the face.

"Did that wake you up!" Babir said surprisingly with a calm smile.

The guard instantly snapped into place, looking at his chief, he was unsure whether to be angry or thankful. He stayed silent and looked out into the distance with a lot more attention.

Yet Babir still felt that his attitude towards his task was ingenuine and it made Babir's blood boil.

"Say, you didn't happen to let a boy and his uncle visiting their relatives' wedding through these gates, around summer time I believe."

The guard looked down to think, admiring the blade closely.

"I don't really know, I think i saw something like that but i'm pretty sure I let them through."

"You don't know? Did you not keep a record like you are supposed to."

"Yeah, sorry about that, I didn't think it was that important."

"Oh really! Also, did you find it strange how you saw me coming from the north but never there? Like, did we travel there by magic or perhaps-" Babir prolonged the last word, smiling as he saw the realisation of the guard slowly surface.

He looked at Babir with frightened eyes and spilled out.

"Oooh, I'm so sorry! I thought-"

"You're out!" Babir's expression turned dead and his smile did a one-eighty.

The guard fell against Babir and begun to beg, Babir just pushed him and shouted.

"A guard that does not pay attention and neither keeps a record, does not take his job seriously, and a man that does not take his job seriously does not deserve that job!! I can't believe you were made the vice-chief! It is an insult to both my men and this fortress! I hope that when I strip you of your rank you can think about what you've done and hope that another service will accept you! Cause i sure won't!"

Nothing more was needed to be said to what happened next with the guard. After collecting his things he was seen walking south towards the 'City-by-the-Sea.' His face towards the ground and his pace timid. Whilst the others booed at the guard, Babir stood smiling and fulfilled.

He turned around and walked back to his quarters, knowing..

That he had gotten his sweet revenge.

MARIA SHEVEL AWARD - 2017

THE MARIA SHEVEL PRIZE was established for the second time this year. The prize is awarded to contestants in the Literature Category for works focused on children's topic and written in any language or genre.

    Maria Shevel is a Ukrainian architect (b. May 1st 1943). After graduation she departed for Central Asia to participate in the construction of the Toktogul hydroelectric power plant in Kyrgyzstan. Afterwards, in 1965, she began working under the direction of Sharf Rashidov's personal administration team in the development of the Hungry Steppe and the architectural layout of Dzhizzak city in Uzbekistan. She received numerous state awards for her work, such as the Hero of Social Labour, Retired Worker and the Motherhood medal.

ABOUT AUTHOR

As a child psychiatrist, **Kamran Salayev** know how keenly children and adolescents feel injustice. They are vainly looking for answers to questions that adults are avoiding. And once they despair and can become easy prey for soul catchers. Then the cruelest and most radical decisions can seem the only true ones.

Kamran graduated from the medical university in Azerbaijan, and then he did is PhD in Japan. Always been interested in art since childhood. In 2013 he wrote is first story for children. Last year, is second story "Elish and Wcker Tales" won Maria Shevel prize as the best work for children (OEBF).

ABOUT TRANSLATOR & ILLUSTRATOR

Timur Akhmedjanov, an British teenager of Uzbek origin, currently lives with his parents in Aldbury village, Hertfordshire, United Kingdom. Growing up in a creative and well-travelled family has inspired him to become a member of the Eurasian Creative Guild, as well as a volunteer for the Open Eurasia Literature Festival and Book Forum. He has a passion for drawing, music, making films, and in the future he wants to become a cinematographer. The biggest influence on his creative life is owed to his grandmother, who was a famous town planner in Uzbekistan, along with his parents who are publishing professionals and leading figures in Europe's Eurasian community.

This is his second project for *Maria Shevel Prize*, Timur previously translated and illustrated *Menik* story by Yakutian writer Ogdo.